TIME OF THE PICTS

A Time Travel Romance

JANE STAIN

janestain.com

FOREWORD

Time of the Picts is not a standalone novel. It's the second book of two that must be read in order. Please read the first book first: Time of the Celts.

Pictish Brooch - St Ninian's Isle Treasure - Photo by Johnbod - Own work, CC BY-SA 3.0, https://common-s.wikimedia.org/w/index.php?curid=15614246

Mousa Broch, Shetland, Scotland - the best surviving example of a broch. Interior:

Photos by Otter - Own work, CC BY-SA 3.0, https://commons.wikimedia.org/w/index.php?curid=4636610B https://commons.wikimedia.org/w/index.php?curid=4636622

❦

I wanted to include in this book various portrayals of Picts, but the owners of these paintings would not give permission. To see what I wanted to share with you, please search online:

1. Detail of a Pictish Cross slab that shows a Pict wearing 'Pictish trousers'

2. The British Museum: A 'Pict' warrior; nude, body stained and painted with birds, animals and serpents carrying shield and man's head, with scimitar

3. The True Picture of a Woman Pict by Laemeur on Deviant Art, of which he says: "This drawing is for my wife, whose extraction traces into the mist-veiled marshes of Pictland, and who thought it would be a hoot to have a picture of herself cast as a sort-of mythic warrior princess. For an example, she showed me a hand-colored engraving by Theodor de Bry which was published in 1590 in an illustrated edition of A Brief and True Report of the New Found Land of Virginia, by Thomas Heriot. I thought the engraving was marvelous, and wanted straight away to do an homage to it. De Bry's engravings were based on a number of watercolors by John White, whose vision of the ancient Picts is about 5% history, and 95% imagination — but what a fun fabrication he came up with! While my version of his "true picture" is still complete fantasy, I did do

away with White's griffon-heads and star-pasties and instead tattooed my model with a mixture of genuine Pictish symbols, iron-age Celtic ornament, and some Scythian bits and bobs."

Jane

CHAPTER 1

Jaelle sat shocked as Richard paid his bill and got up and left, looking smugly over his shoulder at her as he went through the door. Why did Richard's museum exhibit include a stone carved with a stick figure of John with his unique sword?

She had been with John all these years as he developed that sword and seen countless other people be amazed and amused at it. That was John, no doubt about it.

Why was that stone in with historical stuff about Hadrian's Wall? It had to be a trick of some kind. John must have contacted Richard and given him the stone. John knew Richard sometimes put up exhibits at the museum...

Vivian came over on the pretense of refilling Jaelle's coffee, but while she was bending over to do so she put her mouth close to Jaelle's ear and spoke softly, punctuated by the popping of her gum.

"Is everything alright? You look a little upset."

The waitress was fast becoming her only female friend nearby, and Jaelle did her best to avoid lying to her.

"I'm not really sure."

Vivian's motherly frown of worry showed itself for a moment before she schooled it into her normal cheerful waitress face.

"Yeah, I can see that. Well, you know I'm always here if you need me."

When Vivian started to leave, Jaelle stopped her with a question.

"What about my check?"

Vivian shrugged with one of those comical smiles that had been cheering Jaelle up over the last six months since John left her — not quite at the altar, but almost. And then she nodded toward where Richard had just left.

"Bossy Guy there paid for yours, too. At least something good came out of seeing him today, right?"

Jaelle scrunched up her face to show that she wasn't sure about that either, and got up to go to work.

Vivian gave her shoulder a pat, and then apparently unsatisfied with that, moved in close for a sideways hug before she went back to refilling other people's coffee.

"Like I said, I'm always here if you need me."

"Thanks, Viv."

Jaelle looked at her phone for the time and then ran out the door.

Shoot, sitting and gabbing with Richard had almost made her late, and apparently she had just been out "sick" for almost a week, if this morning's headache and the date on her phone and a weird text from Amber made any sense out of anything.

'All OK. I told them you had the flu and would be in as soon as you could.'

Time to quit stocking her fridge with beer. She almost always messed up when she indulged at home, but it was hard to believe she had blacked out an entire week! Anyway, Jan was going to be upset.

Timing the cars just right, Jaelle ran across the boulevard.

But why would John give Richard that stone? What would be the point? He was the one who broke up with her, saying 'Sorry, but we've just grown apart, and Regan is more in tune with me now.'

Jaelle and John were water under the bridge. She'd been priding herself this morning at being over John — until Richard showed her that picture of John on a stone carving.

She ran up the steps to the museum's small locker room, changed into her long green tour-guide uniform, clocked in, and waved at Jan in her office.

Good, Jan didn't look angry at her for missing almost a week of work, just relieved to see she had made it in today.

The last thing Jaelle needed was to lose her job on top of losing John. Just the thought made her shudder. She hurried down to the front desk to pick up her first tour, determined not to garner any complaints about keeping them waiting.

But when she rounded the last corner and saw Richard adding the finishing touches to his Hadrian's Wall exhibit, she felt oddly drawn to it. Against her better judgment, she paused and looked it all over. He had actual stones from the wall, as well as some weapons found on site. It was all fascinating.

But one stone in particular drew her eyes like nothing else ever had.

No.

It couldn't be.

That had only been a dream.

She stepped right up to the stone and put her fingers in the grooves of designs she herself had made with a nail file. And admitted the incontrovertible truth. She hadn't just dreamed it. She had really made these designs. Now that she took notice, there were small nicks still in her fingers from doing this.

So it was real.

I was there.

John is there.

And Breth is real!

A wave of pure joy washed over her at this startling turn of events. He's real. The exquisite specimen of a man who she'd fought beside the past few days was real.

She hadn't just dreamed him into existence. He was a living breathing man who went about naked, wearing only woad painted creatures who animated whenever his muscles moved... Oh, that body. Oh, those blue eyes like deep pools, washing her mind clean with his conscientious regard...

And then pure panic seized her.

How on earth is Breth? Did Nechtan get him after I left?

No.

No, I refuse to believe that. Breth must be wondering where I am. I hope he doesn't think I left on purpose! I need to get back there.

At the sight of Richard coming over with a disturbing look on his face as if he knew the whole story somehow and was coming over to gloat about it, she took off running toward the front desk, calling out to the group of tourists waiting for her.

"Sorry I'm late! I'll give you extra-long tour to make up for it!"

She was met with cheers as she slid to a stop on the glossy museum floor and waved her arms to avoid falling. She hammed it up, really waving her arms wide in order to make the museum patrons laugh — and keep them happy. At least she was good at her job. She did her best to concentrate on that until she could drop this tour off at the museum's gift shop and run back up to Jan's office with a big smile on her face.

"Jan, I know I just had a sick week—"

But Jan dropped the paper she was working on to her desk, pulled off her reading glasses, and gave Jaelle an incredulous look.

"No way, Jaelle. Marie is on vacation this week, and we need you. I let your little week-long 'sick time' slide with the understanding that when you came back, I'd be able to count on you. Whatever it is you're wanting to run off and do, it will have to wait until Marie's back, and then you'll have Monday-Tuesday off as usual."

With every word Jan said, Jaelle felt a little more of her excitement drain out of her, until at the end she was filled with dread. She couldn't get fired. She wouldn't be able to get another job, which would mean moving back in with her parents. Which would be the end of her world.

A hurt look showed on her boss's face for just a moment, reminding Jaelle of the day Jan had hired her.

❧

SEVEN YEARS, SIX WEEKS, AND THREE DAYS AGO — ON her 16th birthday — Jaelle had timidly crept up to this very same office, resume in hand and hope in heart. She was finally old enough. She could pick out her own clothes. Get her hair cut the way she wanted. Wear makeup. She could if she got a job and made her own money. Her parents had said so. She still couldn't believe it.

"Uh, excuse me, but... Are you the manager?"

The woman peering through her glasses at the papers on the desk was younger than Mother, but not by much. At first she looked stern and strict like Mother, but then she took off her glasses and looked up at Jaelle. And smiled just the tiniest bit as she reached out toward Jaelle's resume.

"Yes, I'm Jan Seward, the museum's manager. And you are?"

She handed it to her, meaning to just introduce herself, but as it was wont to do, her mouth said way more than she had in mind.

"I'm Jaelle Penzag, and today is my 16th birthday. I'm big for my age... Well, I guess I'm just big, now that I'm full grown..." Ug! Why did her mouth have to go embarrassing her all the time?

Fortunately, Jan didn't laugh.

"Have you come to apply for the front desk job?"

Jaelle took a deep breath like her friend Amber had advised her to do before explaining where she was coming from.

"I will if you want me to, but the job I really want is the tour guide one—"

At this, Jan grimaced and visibly prepared to let Jaelle down, just as she had feared.

But Jaelle rushed into her explanation, a speech she had been preparing for the past three years.

"I get all A's in history, and every week I read at least one library book from the history section — not the children's history section, the grown-up one. I have wanted to

7

be a tour guide here since I was 13, and to prove it, I've selected all my history reading from the ancient history section, because I know this is the ancient history library. I've been on the tour myself every year for my birthday for the past three years, and I come twice every time you have a free day. I know everything on exhibit here. You can take me around and ask me questions, and I'll tell you all the answers. I could even take you on a tour myself, to prove to you that I can do it."

Jan stood up with a skeptical smile and gestured out toward the museum at large.

"Okay, you're on. This is something I have to see."

Jaelle shook her fists up and down, she was so excited.

"And that's not all. My parents and I are fighting members of the Society for Creative Anachronism with Cinnead Brodie. He says he demonstrates weapons here sometimes, and I would love to help him..."

❧

JAN HAD TAKEN HER IN AND TRUSTED HER WITH more responsibility than any 16-year-old should have had. She had given Jaelle nothing but respect, and Jaelle was trying to take that for granted. She owed the woman much more than that.

Jaelle let her remorse show on her face and appealed to Jan with her eyes. She wanted to reach out and touch the woman's arm the way she used to do when she was younger, but her gut told her that would be going over the line into emotional manipulation, so she didn't, raising her hand up to push her hair out of her eyes instead.

"I'm sorry. Really sorry, okay? You're right. It can wait till Monday."

Jan heaved a sigh of relief and put her glasses back on as she turned back toward her desk and picked up her paper, putting on that stern look that Jaelle now realized was just an act.

"See that it does, Jaelle."

Walking back down to the front desk to pick up the next tour felt like swimming through molasses. It was only 10:30 on Wednesday. She had five whole days of this to endure before she could go back to Breth. It wasn't fair.

She nearly jumped out of her skin when Cinnead tapped her on the shoulder.

"Where have you been all week? It's bad enough these bones are old, now they're rusty, too."

She smiled at her sparring partner — who also happened to be the museum's janitor — as she walked by him, rushing to her next tour so she wouldn't be late.

"You wouldn't believe me if I told you."

CHAPTER 2

Richard sighed impatiently as the horse-drawn carriage took him home from the museum. It was so tedious being here in the city. And the horse was barely giving him any energy. He would get so much more if he could ride the horse. In fact, at every instant he had to stop himself from leaping out of the carriage onto the horse's back. For the time being, he couldn't afford to make a scene. Had to conform to convention.

So tedious.

And yet this open carriage ride was a thousand times better than the museum itself. So artificial. So full of man-made materials and once-natural matter so mangled from its pristine state that it cried out to him in agony, begging him to release it from its torture. Glass that should be sand. Countless metal objects that should be ore in the ground. Even the stone had been ground into a powder and mixed with glue in order to make concrete. Being there drained him.

It was exhausting. Yet he had to finish putting up the exhibit before he left. Convention again. And the museum would be the most likely place for him to discover where the woman lived. He had to remember to get chummy with the receptionist.

He shuddered and leaned toward the horse to get an infinitesimal increase in the natural effect coming off the creature.

After what was too long a ride, the carriage pulled up in front of his apartment building. The realtor had sighed with admiration when he showed it to Richard, so he supposed it was nice. To him, it was just more butchered wood and stone, more burned metal, and more melted sand. But it sure cost a lot of money. Good thing man was so hung up on his past. Exhibits paid well.

At least the doorman — Reese, was it? — had the sense to recognize him in time to rush up and open the carriage door for him before he finished paying the driver.

"Evening, Mr. Caledon."

Richard knew many people learned the names of those who serve them every day, but he thought that was foolish and frivolous. Still, his mother had instilled in him her rather middle-class sense of "good manners."

So he nodded at Reese before allowing the man to open the front door for him, and when the man called the elevator, and again when he pushed the penthouse floor button.

Finally, the elevator doors closed and he was rid of the obligation.

And then they opened, and he relaxed into the splendid atmosphere of his custom-made rooftop green-house apartment. His body thrilled with energy at every step he took on the grass, every pass of a tree branch across his chest and over his arm, every tickle of bush or flower on his legs.

Ah.

It would take all night just to undo the damage done from being in that man-made monstrosity all day. But he needed to more than undo the damage. He needed to build up energy. To be ready. Just in case. The woman was nobody here, but she wasn't without resources.

As he always did, despite how sure he was of the time, he consulted the calendar made of standing stones in his garden. Went into the center and looked to the keystone just as the setting sun found its mark. And nodded to himself in satisfaction. It was almost time. And he would have what he needed.

After removing all of his clothing, he lay on the grass around the largest tree, then them touch as much of his body as possible while he sang the ritual.

🙙

WHEN SHE FINALLY GOT HOME, JAELLE CALLED Amber.

Her friend answered before Jaelle even heard it ring.

"You escaped! How did you do it?"

Jaelle told her, right up to waking up in her house today. She was about to tell how Richard had stolen the helmet, but Amber kept interrupting. As usual.

"Wait. So the helmet wasn't on you? It was in the bag that he hit you with? But you woke up and it was on you?"

Also as usual, Jaelle's friend's interruptions annoyed her. But just a little. Mostly she was glad to have a familiar voice to talk to.

"Amber, if a helmet can take me back and forth in time 2000 years, what's so strange about it being able to pop onto my head in the transition? And anyway, that isn't the point..."

"Where is the helmet, by the way?"

"Back in its box in the basement, in front of the washer."

"Shouldn't you lock it up or something? It's pretty valuable."

"You mean in a safe deposit box?"

"No, no. Keep it at home where you can get to it easily. But it's an antique. It would suck if some thief took it just because of that. Don't you have a home safe?"

"Are you kidding? I'm as poor as they come, Amber. It isn't easy paying this rent on my own, you know. But I see something that may work. Hold on."

"What is it?"

Jaelle laughed at that despite being slightly annoyed. Amber was not a patient person.

"Perfect, it will work. It's John's motorcycle chain. I've chained the helmet to one of the support columns here in the basement. It isn't going anywhere unless I unlock it."

"What if the thief just gets the keys from your purse while you're sleeping?"

"Ha! It's a combination lock."

"Oh good. Now tell me what happened today. That sounded like it was going to be good."

But Jaelle wasn't a minute back into her story before Amber interrupted again.

"Oh come on, Jaelle. There's no way you know for sure that was John just from a stick figure carving on a stone."

Jaelle rolled her eyes before she realized Amber couldn't see her.

"You haven't seen the sword he made. It's like nothing you would ever imagine — and nothing they would have the technology to make during that time. Which is funny, because it's supposed to be a period piece. He made it for his SCA persona. Do you know the SCA are a lot more historically accurate than we were at the faire—"

"Okay, okay. So it's John. He's there in the time of the Celts. But Jaelle, so is Breth. So why are you here in our time? I mean, if you just paused long enough to call me and tell me, thank you. But Kelsey will take me into your dream later on tonight like always. So get off the phone and go to him already. Breth, that is. Go to Breth."

Jaelle loved Amber. The quirky woman was one of her oldest friends and usually understood her. But truth to tell, she wasn't very bright.

"Amber, I can't just quit my job and go rushing off to Breth. Not without a commitment from him that he's going to let me join his family so that I have a place to stay... And it's way too soon for that. I just met him."

Amber laughed.

"Yeah, you're right. You did just meet him. What am I talking about? It was so cool, though, watching you hang out with a blue-painted naked dude — oh, and seeing the inside of a functioning broch. But mostly the naked dude. So good looking, too!"

Jaelle heaved a heavy sigh.

"Tell me about it. I have to wait four more days before I can go see him. Lucky you, you have your man right there. In fact, what are you doing on the phone with me for so long? You should be with Tomas."

It was Amber's turn to sigh, and she did so with such drama that both women laughed some more.

"Tomas has a lot of work to do. I put off coming down here to Australia as long as I could when I was trying to help you, but—"

"Oh! Did you and Kelsey find out anything about the impending battles?"

Amber groaned.

"Jaelle, all the surviving records are Roman, so they are biased. You know that, right?"

"Yeah, yeah, I do. So did you find anything?"

"Well, we did find some stuff. It's not good news."

"Amber, I know you didn't find out he dies anytime soon, or you wouldn't be telling me to rush off to him."

"Very funny. You know Breth's not in the historical records at all, right?"

"I assumed."

Amber cleared her throat again, an unconscious habit that was a sure sign she didn't want to be in the conversation.

"There are no heavy Pictish casualties in Breth's period of time. The cleansing, as the Romans call it, came centuries later, so the news is semi good."

There was more. Jaelle could tell. So she kept from saying anything, just let the silence bear down on Amber, knowing it would force her to speak. It took almost a minute, which is a long time on the phone, but it worked.

"That particular broch Breth's clan is in, it's really close to the wall. There aren't any so close in our time. It's not there anymore."

Bile rose up in Jaelle's throat, and she ran into the kitchen for a glass of water and chugged it, then gasped for air.

"Well, he says he doesn't stay there very much. They move around a lot from broch to broch, like nomads. And you know it could have been destroyed centuries into Breth's future."

"Right. Yeah, you're right. The histories we read don't say when it got destroyed."

"You know what? Don't look that up."

"Wasn't going to."

"Well, tell me about Australia."

Amber gave a small squeal of delight.

"The down-under faire doesn't start for another two weeks, but Tomas is really busy doing the advertising and getting vendor contracts signed. Dall does most of that now, but he's teaching Tomas so he can take over soon..."

For the rest of the conversation — which lasted several hours, during which she ate dinner and took a bath – Jaelle encouraged Amber to speak about her new life. She knew most of the people Amber mentioned, so it was comforting to hear what they were up to. But mostly it just got her mind off waiting to go see Breth.

CHAPTER 3

Jaelle had to drag herself to work each day. All she wanted to do was put on the helmet and return to Breth. But it would be foolish to throw away her job just to rush off and see someone she'd only known a week. So she dutifully showed up each day and did her best to be entertaining with the patrons.

Sparring with Cinnead wasn't the bright spot in her routine that it once had been. It seemed too easy. He had a hole in his guard. How had she not noticed before? He was huffing and puffing for breath much sooner than usual, too. She didn't say anything in front of the museum patrons, but when she saw him in the breakroom, she signaled they should go for a walk down into the basement storage, where no one would overhear.

"I know you said while I was gone for a week you got out of practice, but what's really going on? Your technique is much sloppier than usual."

"Are you kidding? Your technique is much sharper than usual."

"It is?"

"Aye, it is. And you're faster. And you have new moves. Almost as if you went on a trip to get extra training this last week instead of having the flu."

He gave her a significant look and crossed his arms, leaning back on the counter, obviously waiting for an explanation.

And she really liked Cinnead. She owed him a lot, too.

She was tempted to tell him a tall tale about some secret training camp. That would explain everything so easily. But she had been cautioned about what happened when you told a lie. Something about a tangled web... Well anyway, once you told one lie, you ended up telling so many you couldn't keep them straight. Best to stick with the truth as much as possible.

She racked her brain. What could she tell him?

But while she did so, her mouth took off on its own again. She thanked the lord above it didn't blurt out the whole story.

"All I can say is I wasn't really sick. You're right. I did get some training—"

He looked so eager, it broke her heart.

"I knew it. Where? They're obviously good. Was it expensive? Well, even if it was, I have some savings."

She tried her hardest to show him empathy and not pity on her face.

"They don't take just anyone. You need a referral, and I'm not qualified to give one, never will be."

There was no way he could go. No way he'd be able to keep up.

۶

THE SUN WOKE RICHARD AS USUAL SUNDAY morning. Good. All the damage had been undone and he still had time to build up some energy. He grasped the tree as tightly as he could and sang as fast as he could until he was out of time and simply had to stop in order to have time to shower and dress before he ran out the door to catch the carriage the morning doorman knew to call for him.

These morning rides weren't nearly so bad as the evening rides.

He peeked into the diner casually, as he walked by its glass door. Good, the woman wasn't here yet. He went in and got the meal the doorman had ordered for him, then hurried across the all but deserted street and up into the hideously huge and polished building.

He had long since finished eating and was congratulating himself on getting the exhibit half ready in half a week when who should enter through the front door but Professor Smerty, carrying a large suitcase. Richard had to concentrate not to see the man in his lecturing robes.

Looking quite fit and happy for an old gray-hair,

Smerty sauntered up to the front desk and gave the girl a pleasant smile.

"Excuse me, Miss."

The receptionist's eyes widened as she took in the man's presence.

"Yes?"

Smerty reached out his hand to shake the girl's.

"I'm Alasdair, the archaeologist from Celtic University, reporting in for my foremaist day o work. Sorry tae be late, but my flight was delayed." He lifted his suitcase so she could see it.

Blast! That Jaelle woman had connections she obviously didn't appreciate, if they could get Smerty here. She entered the lobby next, plainly not knowing who Smerty was. Ignoring him, in fact.

Richard ran to the men's room. Once he had put five man-made walls between himself and Smerty, Richard used up all the extra energy from the tree and the grass and the bushes — in order to cast illusion on himself specific and only to Smerty's vision — and avoid being recognized.

🐎

JAELLE WATCHED IN ASTONISHMENT AS RICHARD took off running toward the men's room. And then she smiled. That man deserved to have the runs. He was so...

Presumptuous?

No.

Aloof?

No.

Ooh, I know. Condescending.

She was walking past Reception to pick up her next tour group when the old man at the counter stuck his hand out, eager to shake.

"Hello. I'm Alasdair Smerty, the new archaeologist. It's my foremaist day. And ye are?"

Whoa, Smerty dude. Archaeologists don't need to shake hands with tour guides. And you're giving off the strangest vibe.

And he was. Even with his grey hair and gnarled hands, he had the air of the warrior. Creepy didn't begin to cover it.

The hairs on the back of her neck stood up. She was not getting close enough for him to grab her hand — which she was sure he would do, given the opportunity. His stance was ready for a lunge. She put her hands up in a helpless gesture and nodded toward her group, then spoke quickly as she rushed past him.

"Hello. I'm Jaelle Penzag, one of the tour guides, and I'm needed over there. Please excuse me."

Feh. Her hackles raised as she passed by. It was all she could do not to shudder. She safely got to her tour group and thought that was the end of it.

But the creepy old guy didn't give up.

At lunch, he was standing around the edge of the break room when she came in, only coming to sit down after she had – right next to her.

Thank goodness there were other people around.

He even tried to pass her a note.

She pointedly ignored it, concentrating on eating her lunch and listening to what Jan had to say about the plans for next year's charity gala. Jan was a good chaperone. Jaelle scooted her chair a little closer to the familiar woman and pointedly did not look in Alasdair's direction.

Once more, she thought that would be the end of it.

And once more, it wasn't.

When it was time to go home, he ran out and walked next to her, smiling at Jan and Cinnead at just the right moments to seem friendly and not stalkery.

"I'll walk ye to yer car."

This was ridiculous. Should she threaten him? She would if he touched her. She didn't have a weapon, but she knew a few karate moves. Just a few.

"Oh, I don't have a car. I take the bus. The stop is pretty far. You should just go to your own car. Really."

She walked a little faster, hoping his legs wouldn't be up to her speed, but no such luck. In fact, her luck seemed to be getting worse.

He hustled to stay beside her.

"Ye shouldna hae to take the bus. I'll give ye a lift. My car's parked over thataway."

Enough already! Indignation surged through her.

Without stopping or even slowing down, she managed to turn her head toward him and give him a derisive look.

"I don't take rides from strangers. I don't know where

you're from, but around here you won't find many women who will."

Man oh Manischewitz, why hadn't she raised her voice when she said that? This man shouldn't work at the museum. He was clearly a predator. And now when his body was found, it would seem as if she were the aggressor. Better yell.

But when she turned to do that, she saw that her luck had changed. Finally.

Looking deflated, he was letting her walk on without him. But he called out after her in one last pathetic effort to get her to go with him. The audacity.

"I think ye wull be interested in what I have tae say."

At that, Jaelle allowed herself to break into a flat-out run to the bus stop, praying the whole time the bus would come soon and Alasdair wouldn't drive by in his car. For some reason, she just didn't think she could take that.

But her new good luck held. The bus did come soon.

Once she got on, she didn't stop to think about where Alasdair Smerty might be from, who had sent him, or why. She didn't care, just dismissed him as someone else's problem. Because she was on her way to see Breth again.

One agonizingly long bus ride later, she was home. Where the helmet was. Her ticket back to Breth!

Eagerly, she ran down to the basement, changed into the knee-length plaid sheath dress from his time, and went to put on the helmet.

But then she stopped. Grabbing a large purse — a leather one that could pass for a period piece — she shoved in anything she could think of that she might need: Tampons, check. Swiss Army knife, check. Matches, check...

A dozen more items later, she was back to the helmet and putting it on, indescribably excited to be seeing Breth again.

CHAPTER 4

Breth enjoyed using the new fighting moves Jaelle had shown them. Practice truly was fun again now, as much fun as it had been when he was young and eager. Perhaps even more so.

The clan won most of their battles now. It was really helping. It was a kind favor the druids of the future had given him ... him and the rest of the clan. He was glad she'd been here.

Breth ducked as Talorac lunged straight for his face, laughing as Jaelle used to do when she did the same move.

He winked at his brother.

Well done. That move is anything but new to us anymore, but it sure is new and dangerous to the barbarian invaders, aye?"

"Aye, the moves all work a charm, don't they?"

"Aye."

The two of them smiled at each other awkwardly.

Everyone knew Breth would rather Jaelle were here than just her sword moves.

Breth was moving on to his next bout partner when his mother drew near with her hand on her chin, a sign that she wanted to have a word but wasn't going to use her authority as the clan's planning chief's wife in order to be obvious about summoning him. Not in front of the other clans who were gathered all around, practicing and gathering and herding along with his clan.

Asking with his eyes if anything was amiss, he made his way over to her.

She shook her head the tiniest bit to reassure him, and the two of them walked off by themselves in the direction of the sacred grove.

The broch was nice and all, but the sacred grove was home. He would miss it. He always did.

But right now in the moment, Mother had put a tender hand on his forearm, loving as always, and seemingly meek and mild.

But he knew better. Automatically, his emotional guard came up. Good thing, too, because she cut straight to his heart.

"Even if she does come back, she won't find us after we move on tomorrow. Perhaps you should move on as well. Go ahead and marry Morna this Beltane. And mind you, marriage is not something you spring on a woman at the last moment, understand? Give her time to send for her mother."

The two of them walked on in silence awhile, Breth watching his feet form footprints and feeling such sadness that he couldn't bear it. When he spoke, it was to get his mind off yearning for someone who wasn't here.

"Very well. I'll speak with Morna this evening."

There was Mother's oh-so-gentle hand again on his forearm, ostensibly in sympathy.

But he knew better. It was really the caress she gave him as a reward for doing her bidding. As if he were six again. Once a mother, always a mother.

She walked off then, back toward the broch still looking at him significantly, her look that said 'You said you would, better do it now.' She didn't add the 'or else' look she had used when he was a child, but he saw it anyway in her posture.

He sighed with reluctance.

But she was right.

He may as well go and ask Morna to be his bride. He needed children, and his clan would benefit from an alliance with hers. He would do it for the good of his clan.

He knew just who he would find her with, too. She wasn't a fighter like Jaelle. Morna was more 'the gathering type,' she called it.

He knew better.

She liked to be in the company of other women so she could gossip.

He asked around and was told the gatherers were inside the broch, packing up supplies for tomorrow's trek.

❧

Jaelle woke up lying down in the same spot where she had arrived last time, deep in the woods a few miles north of Hadrian's Wall and a few miles south of Breth's broch. She took off the helmet, carefully stowed it in its bag under her sword belt, and looked around, breathing deep and smiling her biggest smile.

She made it!

And she had her purse this time. All the comforts of home.

She put it on her shoulder and headed toward Breth.

❧

Breth was waiting for the guard to open the broch's door for him when Talorac called his name, pointing up into the hills.

Breth turned and looked and nearly fainted.

Jaelle's spirit was descending toward the broch.

He shed a tear for her. But that was not the way, and he quickly quenched his sadness in favor of practicality. He would stay awake in her honor tomorrow night, as tonight was the clan meeting.

But why did her spirit have to come all the way back here in the afterlife to pester him? He would welcome it, of course. Would let the spirit stay as long as it wanted in order to be with her in the only way he could...

Despite a lifetime of denying himself grief for the

dead, in this case he felt sorry for himself. Why did she have to come as a spirit? It would be torture for him. Pure torture. He wanted from her what a spirit couldn't give.

And he didn't mean children.

He stood there motionless, unable to move or even think as he watched her come down the hill.

Even in spirit form, she moved with a fighter's grace. He couldn't help admiring her. Now accustomed to the idea of shortish hair on a woman, he gazed on the curly brown cloud around her head with affection.

At long last she was with him, and he imagined he could smell her musky scent.

He had it bad.

"Spirit of my lost Jaelle, I welcome you." He took his eyes off her and lowered his head in submission, showing her she had no reason to use any of those spirit hijinks everyone so dreaded. He particularly didn't fancy being hit from behind with things when the spirit briefly animated to throw them.

He chuckled a little. That would be just like her. Maybe it wouldn't be so bad...

She spoke to him in a way that at first confused him.

"I'm not a spirit. I'm here, Breth."

His confusion was cast aside when she grabbed him and kissed him heartily. Could it be? Doubt fled his mind quickly, and soon he was grabbing her in turn, and kissing her just as heartily.

Ten clans were here for the chieftain meeting, so the

place was crowded – and everyone cheered at the show the two of them were putting on.

He relaxed into it.

Until Morna came storming out of the broch. She must've heard the cheering.

He really couldn't care less.

But Morna asserted herself well. And if he were kissing anyone but Jaelle, he would've been impressed with the spunkiness Morna showed in the face of competition. Might have even come to love Morna a little bit.

"Breth, you're making a huge mistake, and I can forgive you for it if you stop now. But if you carry on like this, then I am going to make your life miserable. Now–"

He intended to address Morna's outburst himself, but Jaelle beat him to it, simply amazing him even more.

"You won't be making his life miserable, and if you don't back down and apologize right now, I will see that you're never near him again."

Morna's face was comically shocked, and for a moment she was speechless – something he had never seen before, and he'd known Morna all her life. She rallied, unfortunately, putting her hands on her hips and sneering at Jaelle.

"What? How are you going to have the power to make sure I'm never near him again?"

Jaelle put her arm around him possessively and drew herself close to him, putting her other hand on his chest like the submissive woman she definitely was not.

He had to bite his lip to keep from laughing.

She lifted her chin and spoke down her nose at Morna.

"Power as his wife, fool."

What?

He opened his mouth to ask Jaelle, 'Don't I have a say in this?' But when his eyes met hers, he realized he agreed completely. He wanted her as his wife. There was no question about it in his mind at all, so he just shrugged and kissed her some more.

But Morna huffed and trudged off toward the sacred grove, where the clan chiefs' meeting was to be held this evening.

"We'll see about that."

Smiling at everyone, Breth grabbed his woman close to him and led her away from the crowd, who looked and sounded all too eager to share in his happiness. He wouldn't mind an audience, but she was oddly prude and shy, she had only just returned to him, and he didn't want her running off again.

And she felt indescribably good up against him.

But she froze.

"Where's Nechtan? You are aware you can't trust him, right? I mean, I know he's one of the clan's Druids and everything, but —"

"I assure you Nechtan won't be bothering anyone anymore. And I am so sorry I didn't rid the world of him sooner, the first time he affronted you. Please say you forgive me."

"Of course I forgive you. Yeah."

Holding her as tight as he could while still walking, he asked her the question that was most on his mind — now that he knew she lived.

"Where have you been for two moon cycles?"

She gave him a puzzled face as they walked and held each other.

"What do you mean? I've only been gone five days."

"Maybe for you it's been five days, but here... So much has gone on, I don't know where to start. There's a new barbarian commander at the fort, some foreign chieftain is bent on uniting all of our clans, and you got here mere seconds before I asked Morna to marry me."

She hugged him fiercely.

Smiling at that, he responded in kind, holding as much of her body to him as he possibly could.

The temptation to stop and make full-on love to her — right here on the ground in front of everyone — was so strong, the only way he resisted it was to keep putting one foot in front of the other. Only once he was successful at resisting his strongest urge did the implications of what she had said come to his mind. They troubled him.

"I know that helmet can send you home and back again, but if five days in your time means two months in my time, then I cannot have you going back and forth."

Surprising him, she pushed away and walked on her own, looking over her shoulder at him with hurt in her face.

"Breth, I do want to get to know you better – in the real sense. I want to understand what makes you tick and to really be close to you. That's my idea of what being a wife is."

Puzzled at the hurt in her eyes but delighted she felt the same way he did, he went to hold her close again.

"Then let's marry tonight!"

But her hurt look changed to worry, and she pulled away some more.

"In my time, strangers get to know each other for six to twelve moon cycles first, before we marry and commit our lives to each other."

What?

"Jaelle, marriages are arranged here."

Hurt changed to despair in her eyes.

He rushed on to explain.

"We can disagree to an arrangement. We don't have to accept it. I was going to agree to Mother's arrangement with Morna's mother for the sake of my clan. An alliance with her clan – which is a stronger one — would help us greatly."

Her look of despair grew, and so he dropped what he was trying to explain and rushed into coaxing her back into his arms, holding them open for her.

"Anyway, if you're going to live in our time, you'll need to live by our ways."

Good. Her despair fled, replaced by wariness. He was accustomed to wariness. He could work through it.

She crossed her arms, but she turned to face him. And the tiniest smile threatened to break through on her stoic face.

"I don't remember promising to live in your time, Breth. All I said was I wanted to spend more time together to see if this will work."

They were far enough away now that they had privacy, but ironically, now he didn't feel like taking advantage of it by laying her gently on the grass. No, now he just wanted to...

What?

His pride wanted him to do just as he had done the first day they met. 'Walk away,' it said. 'Make her choose to follow you.'

But his heart wasn't sure she would follow this time. It was a problem.

He gave her his most appealing look.

"The chieftain meeting starts soon, and as the fighting leader of my clan, I need to go along with Father and Mother, the planning leaders. I hope you'll stay until it's over so that we can talk. It will end quite late, perhaps even after dawn."

She took a deep breath, probing the depths of his soul with her eyes, whether she knew it or not. Her look cut right to the heart of him. Tempted him to forswear his ways — even to leave with her, go back to her time with her.

And he could admit the idea terrified him. Here, he was capable. In control. Respected. There? Who knew?

But she drew him like no other person ever had. Her sad brown eyes drew him in and promised refuge and peace no matter where they were, so long as they were together.

Gradually, her face softened.

"Yes, I can stay that long. Have a good meeting and I'll see you afterward."

CHAPTER 5

Breth kissed her then. And while their earlier kisses had been desperate and needy and taking, this kiss was giving. It was gentle and soft — and loving. She savored it, drawing it out as long as she could without rekindling the passion that lay just underneath, begging to be let out.

But no kiss could last forever.

He drew away, regret showing in his eyes, but determination and duty more so.

"Ask after my brother Talorac. I leave you to his care while I'm away."

It was on the tip of Jaelle's tongue to tell him she didn't need looking after while he was gone, that she was a grown woman and had been caring for herself these five years, thank you very much.

But then she looked at the hundreds of strangers in

the distance around the broch and realized yes, she did need a protector.

"Are you sure I'll be all right walking back there by myself? Will I be given enough time to ask for Talorac before I'm... waylaid? None of these people know who I am."

As soon as she'd promised to see him later, he had relaxed. And now he smiled a mischievous smile full of playfulness.

"Aw, but they will have seen you walk up here with me. You'll be fine walking over there, but do ask for Talorac. I do not trust the other men around you unless you have part of my clan declaring you ours."

Goosebumps rose all down Jaelle's arms. This possessiveness should have put her off, she knew. But she liked it.

She smiled back at him, wrinkling her nose to show that she could be mischievous too.

"I'm not going to do *everything* you say, you know."

He chuckled at this even as he pulled her close once more and clung to her, rumbling his oh-so-masculine voice near her ear.

"Oh, I can see that very well."

She sighed in pleasure.

"Just so we understand each other."

He pulled away then, letting go of contact with her body one inch at a time, slowly, until the only thing touching were their hands. He squeezed hers, she squeezed back, and then they let go.

She felt the loss immediately.

What was encouraging was he apparently did too. He kept looking at her as he walked backward toward the sacred grove until he started to trip, gave her a self-deprecating smile, and then at last turned around.

And ran.

Startled that he was running, she turned and looked back toward the broch.

And quickly jumped out of the pathway.

Breth's parents and ten other couples their age were running straight at her, along with ten people her and Breth's age.

Not toward her, toward the Sacred Grove.

They all ran past her at an amazing speed and then disappeared around the bend after Breth in a cloud of dust.

Truly at a loss as to what else she could possibly do, she headed toward the broch and inquired of the first person she saw, a woman who was probably her age, judging by the baby in a sling on her stomach, but who looked twice that because of the sun wrinkles on her face. She was holding the hand of a small child as she picked berries and put them in a basket.

Jaelle spoke to her quickly.

"I'm here with Breth. He says Talorac should watch after me while he's at the chieftain meeting. Where is Talorac, please?"

The woman put her hand on her hip.

"Aw, I don't want to leave my spot. Someone else might take it. My son can help you. Galam!"

A boy no older than seven ran up and stopped abruptly, looking up with respect at his mother while not very surreptitiously studying Jaelle — and apparently finding her interesting, as his eyes stayed on her longer than anyone would think polite.

"Yes, Mother?"

The baby started crying, and the woman swung the sling back and forth gently between the branches of the berry bush.

"Galam, take this woman..."

"Oh, sorry. My name's Jaelle."

"Thank you. I'm Arela. Galam, take Jaelle to the practice field. Find Talorac and deliver her to his care, understand?"

Galam nodded eagerly, making his head of red hair bob in the wind.

"Yes, Mother." He looked up at Jaelle. "Where did you come from?"

Firmly clamping her tattletale mouth shut, Jaelle looked down into the small boy's openly curious young face.

At a loss for what to tell him, she appealed to his mother with her eyes, thinking surely this was too rude a question for a child to be asking her.

But no such restriction existed in this time, plainly. Because Arela was looking at Jaelle just as curiously as Galam was.

Jumping Jehoshaphat!

What was she going to tell these people? Her eyes took in the vast crowd around the broch, ten times larger than Breth's clan. All of these people?

A familiar voice cut into her nearly panicked reverie.

"The druids sent her. She's from two thousand years in the future."

Not knowing whether to feel relieved or alarmed, Jaelle turned to look at Breth's brother and gauge his intent.

Talorac regarded her warily, and she couldn't blame him. Two months she'd been gone, after knowing them all just a week.

"I hear you're looking for me."

She swallowed the lump in her throat and looked at the younger man. He would be considered no more than a boy at home, but here he was definitely a man. About 17, he already had the full confidence of a fighter — and the muscle mass.

She forced herself to give Arela and Galam an apologetic look.

"Thank you anyway. It was nice to meet you."

Arela narrowed her eyes to let Jaelle know *she* knew Jaelle was glad to be getting out of their conversation.

"And you too." And then Arela gave Jaelle a pointed stare and added in a too-casual tone, "Will we see you again?"

What a loaded question.

Jaelle smiled her respect at Arela. The woman had chutzpah.

"Honestly? I don't know. But I do hope so."

Arela tipped her head to the side in acknowledgment.

"Well, that's something then, isn't it." She gave Jaelle the tiniest smile before she got back to her berry picking, adjusting the baby's sling so it didn't strain her back so much as she bent over.

Jaelle turned back to Talorac.

He gestured toward the broch.

"Let's get you to safety."

She gave him the briefest nod and started walking, relieved when he fell in beside her, even though she barely knew him.

"I suppose you know Breth wants you to look after me while he's in the meeting."

"Aye, and it's a bit inconvenient. I don't suppose you'll be in much danger inside the broch, though. I could go on about my business then, after leaving word I should be notified if anything happens." He looked at her defiantly.

Oho. Then there wasn't much difference between teens now and teens at home after all. That was oddly reassuring. She'd been starting to think she was on a planet of aliens and not really on Earth at all, seeing Galam show his mother so much respect.

She gave him a conspiratorial smile.

"I suppose that'll be fine. But you know word will get back to Breth. And it won't be me saying anything."

He looked relieved for the briefest second, but then he covered it up with what passed for being cool in this time: standing up straight in a fighting stance and handling the hilt of his sword.

"I'm not afraid of Breth. Anyway, as I said, nothing's going to happen to you in the broch."

And then she remembered the fire.

Quickly, she glanced over, and then sighed in relief. The roof was no longer thatched.

He must've seen where she looked, because he laughed a little.

"What, did you think I was setting you up?"

She gave him her best warrior's appraising look: calm, but the tiniest bit challenging.

"One can never be too careful."

He relaxed a bit and laughed like they were old friends.

"You have a chance with Breth. He plainly prefers you. But you need to stick around, or that won't matter. We men are opportunists when it comes to women." He looked her over. "You're old enough to know that."

By now they were halfway to the broch, and the area was teeming with activity. Fighters were practicing and children were running about playing. Some of them were herding the animals — and Jaelle would have bet they were all supposed to be doing so.

It was another source of unexpected relief, to see that children were pretty much the same always. Though

they really did show their parents a lot more respect to
their faces in this time.

She watched the general hubbub with a growing
sense of peace and belonging. When she'd first shown up
and seen all the extra people, she'd been anxious.
Everyone had stared at her. And then they had seen
Breth watching her and backed off — though not very
confidently.

Now that she was walking with Talorac though, all
these strangers appeared to accept that she wasn't an
enemy. They were not exactly friendly — no one said a
word to her, and they didn't ask Talorac about her.

Breth's brother walked right up to the guard at the
door to the broch.

"Jaelle is a guest of Breth's. She is to be given respect
and provisions, and a place to sleep if she needs it. She
awaits his return."

The guard nodded and turned to open the door.

And Talorac turned to leave.

Jaelle's apprehension surprised her.

Her mouth tried to open and beg him to stay with her
after all.

But she firmly clamped her teeth over her tongue.
She was a big girl. She could take care of herself.

Anyway, Talorac was gone.

The guard gestured her into the vestibule and closed
the outer door after them before he opened the inner
door and called out to the nearest person.

Who happened to be Morna.

Ugh.

"Take heed and please spread the news. This is Breth's guest awaiting his return. She is to be given provisions and a place to sleep if needed."

Against her will, Jaelle turned to follow him back into the vestibule, but he had closed the door already. She was standing in a 30-foot-wide circular room with the woman who might've had Breth, if Jaelle hadn't come along.

Wonderful.

Jaelle looked around to see if there was anybody else in the vicinity.

Thankfully there was. Women were packing up excess bedding and feeding their children. But they pointedly ignored the scene at the door — though they did seem to be moving closer than they needed to in order to perform their various tasks.

Morna looked like the cat who ate the canary.

"If you think I'm going to help you get something to eat or a place to sleep—"

But Jaelle pushed past Morna and turned to the right, then pushed through the door into the stairwell between the two outer walls.

"No problem. I can show myself upstairs. I know where to go."

This did not go over well with Morna at all. She huffed a little bit and struggled to say something scathing.

But she didn't manage to say anything at all before Jaelle was going up the stairs. And then she finally thought of something.

"Don't get too comfortable!"

Hitching up her skirt and basically crawling up the steep narrow stone staircase between the two outer walls, Jaelle laughed all the way to the fourth floor.

And when she went in the door there, she saw just the person she was hoping to see.

CHAPTER 6

Breth loved being here in the Sacred Grove, but he didn't like these meetings with all the chieftains. There was no one clear leader, and that was a problem. No one could indicate it was anyone's turn to speak, so everyone spoke at once. It was maddening.

On Breth's right, Uradech was speaking the loudest.

"We should hear him out. They say he's an amazing fighter and leader. He could unite us all against the invaders."

Four other chieftains called out their agreement.

"We should!"

"Aye!"

"We'd be stronger together!"

"Let's bring the battle to the invaders!"

On Breth's left, Father spoke calmly to Mother, who hung on his every word, nodding in agreement.

"Our clan must remain separate and able to protect ourselves as we see fit. If we join with all the rest of the clans under one leader, how is he going to listen to each and every one of us? He can't. And he'll have so much power, his head will swell. He'll become selfish, even if he didn't start that way."

Breth could see both points of view.

Uradech's voice was growing heated.

"Our voices won't matter one bit when the invaders run the lucky among us into the ground and make the rest their slaves. They already have too many of us. If we unite, we can get our people back and prevent more from being taken."

Father'd had enough. It was evident by the set of his jaw and the clenching of his fists.

Breth looked over to Mother, beseeching her to use her calming touch and prevent Father from dividing the people even more.

But Mother gave Breth her 'quit it' look.

That was when Breth knew. No matter what they said at this meeting, trouble was coming.

Trying to help Father maintain his dignity as a chieftain who didn't lose control of himself, Breth stood up to answer Uradech himself.

But that was the wrong thing to do.

Father put his hand on Breth's shoulder and pulled him down, rising up himself.

Mother gave Breth a reproachful look that he just knew was about him cavorting with Jaelle and spurning

Morna, as much as if not more than about what had just happened. She took her husband's hand, supporting him.

Father pulled mother up to stand beside him.

All this had taken but a moment, and Uradech was still speaking.

Father butted in very forcefully, with all the authority he had in his considerable frame.

"If this sort of unification is forced on my clan, we will leave and become our own people. Each one of us is the only thing in this life. Other people are there for company and for children to further the people, but we each must have a say over our own life, or how are we alive? We are not meant to be tools for someone else to use as he sees fit. Each man and each woman is a life unto his or her own, and all of our lives must be respected always."

Uradech plainly didn't appreciate being interrupted, because all the while, he was yelling to be heard over Father.

"Individual personhood is not something we can consider when the invaders threaten to overrun and annihilate us! People can explore and discover and celebrate their lives in times of peace. In times of war, we all must pull together. The threat is so large that if we don't, there won't be any of us left to celebrate our individual lives..."

Father and Uradech weren't the only ones yelling. Almost everyone was talking at once. Only Breth and a few others were listening.

Even if I jump up and shout for them all to be still, I don't think they will. There must be some way...

Breth hated feeling so helpless. He was usually able to command attention, but with all these chiefs in the room no one could. So he listened. For a long time into the night, he hoped to hear something of use, but no such fortune came. There were definitely two separate camps, and it didn't appear the two could be reconciled.

Which camp should I join?

Stupid question.

No matter what I believe, I'll stay with Father, my strongest tie. And he does have a point. Each of us does have to live our life on our own first and foremost—

All the talking stopped and everyone's head turned toward the path leading up from the river, where a murmur started, making its way slowly over to Breth's side of the grove.

"Drest is coming."

"He's so small."

"What kind of sword is that?"

"He'll unite us."

"Where did he come from?"

"He's so brown and foreign looking."

"Look how many fighters he has with him."

Father's voice boomed in a whisper next to Breth in response to the latest murmur.

"I never thought I'd see any of those never-do-wells again."

"Me neither."

"Nay."

As Drest came up the path from the river, he greeted a few of the chieftains by name and shook forearms with them.

Some turned away from his greeting.

Drest moved to the natural focus spot in the sacred Grove, the place where the Druids usually stood to draw woad clay decorations on the fighters before battle. He stood there and waited while everyone else sat down again, making him not seem so small.

The sword the small brown man carried was... indescribable. Of what sort of metal had it even been made? It looked too heavy for him.

Seeing everyone staring at it, he took it out and made some unusual moves with it that not even Jaelle used — and clearly the sword was not too heavy for him. Again, what was it made of?

And then Drest smiled. It was the smile of someone who knows a secret that is giving him power.

My fighters and I are fighting the fight that you all should be fighting. We're taking it to the Romans. If you join us and we work hard enough, we can keep the Romans out of this area. The area south of that new wall is lost, but the area north of the wall can all be one nation. For right now, you have a choice. You can choose to join with me and receive training in how we fight—"

Uradech called out.

"Will we get weapons like yours?"

Drest regarded Uradech, weighing the man.

"No. I'm sorry I cannot produce any more like it. This is the only one. But the leader of the people should be distinguishable. The people need to have a clear leader to turn to, someone who makes decisions for all, or chaos will prevail. I overheard some of your discussion and I think you know what I mean. You have a week to join me, or I will take you over by force."

After dropping his demand in their laps, Drest turned and walked back down toward the river without any ceremony or farewell, taking all of his men and his amazing sword with him.

The murmuring and arguing started up again as soon as he was out of sight. As before, half the people wanted to unite and half of the people didn't.

"Let's get everyone and take them out. What are we waiting for?"

"That's the stupidest thing I ever heard. With our warriors and his put together, we have more than we need to push those invaders out of our land, demolish their wall, and even see to it they don't multiply anymore."

Breth looked over at Father to see if he was as grieved as Breth was about this division among the people.

But if he was, he wasn't showing it.

CHAPTER 7

Jaelle was relieved to see Deoord look up from where he was sitting with the clan's other druids at the round wooden table where they usually ate with the chieftain, his immediate family, and the messengers.

"Jaelle! I knew you would come back to us. You remember Ia and Boanne."

The female druids nodded at her as he named them.

Jaelle smiled at them and then felt awkward as she stood there waiting to be invited to come sit down. She hoped they weren't having a private meeting, because Morna was undoubtedly one floor up in Breth's room, waiting to give Jaelle a hard time the moment she set foot inside.

And this made her wonder. Had Morna been sharing that room with Breth? He'd said he was about to ask her to be his wife. If the two of them were that close... If there was any chance Morna was carrying Breth's child...

If that's the case, then should I be staying here? I'm an intruder, really.

Her hand went to the helmet.

Gasping, Deoord jumped up and ran over.

"Sorry to keep you standing there. Come on in and sit down. Our home is your home."

Reverently taking her hand, he pulled out the chair between the two female druids.

With a sigh of relief, Jaelle sat down. And got an idea. Would these friendly druids explain why so much time had passed here while she was away, even though time remained the same at home while she was here? But asking would reveal the fact that she knew less about the helmet than she should, if it were designed for her. She'd better come clean about how she was here.

"Thank you for the warm welcome, but..."

She lowered her voice to a whisper, not wanting to admit this to anyone but them. If they told anyone else, that would be their right, of course, but she didn't want anyone else to know if she could help it.

"I need to clear the air about how I got here."

She looked Deoord in the eye.

"You jumped to the conclusion that the druids of my time had sent me, and I let you keep that assumption out of self-preservation. But I know you'll eventually figure out the truth, and so I'm going to tell you, God help me."

At the mention of her God, the three druids sat up

straighter and took a real interest in her, even more so than they had before. Interesting.

She swallowed the lump in her throat.

"It's true that druids control this helmet."

She tapped the bag on her belt, and when Ia and Boanne gave her questioning looks, she took the helmet out and put it on the table.

Ia looked at her with a question in her eyes.

Jaelle carefully slid the helmet across the table to her.

Gingerly, Ia took the helmet in her hands. As soon as she touched it, she jumped a little, as if she'd been shocked. With a look of wonder, she turned the helmet every which way, her smile growing bigger and bigger. Finally, she looked inside. And breathed out and in again as if in ecstasy.

Jaelle jumped up and went behind Ia to see what she was seeing.

"What is it?"

Ia reluctantly handed her the helmet.

"Hold it so the lamp lights the inside, and you'll see the runes."

Jaelle did so.

"What do they say?"

Ia shook her head sadly.

"They were made by Gaels."

Jaelle groaned.

"I can speak Gaelic, but I can't read it."

Boanne turned to Jaelle.

"Does the explanation of why you can speak the

language of the Gaels have anything to do with what you were about to tell us?"

Jaelle gave Boanne a grimacing smile in acknowledgment of her perception.

"Only in a roundabout way. Do you want the long version, or the short?"

Deoord shrugged and looked around him.

"There are many hours before the chieftains will be ready for us to go down to the Sacred Grove and apply the woad for the trek back to their homes. The long version sounds interesting."

Jaelle sat back down again and made herself as comfortable as she could in the face of the reaction she might possibly get now.

Make this good. Give them as much sympathy for you as possible...

"In my time we have fairs where we reenact history—"

Ia excitedly cut her off.

"Most of the clan members don't realize it, but that's what all our gatherings are about too! Instilling our history in the people's memories as if—"

Deoord tapped Ia's shoulder with the back of his hand.

She sighed and shrugged before relaxing back into her seat and gesturing for Jaelle to continue.

Jaelle looked at Boanne, hoping she would butt in too, but no such luck.

"My parents were big historical reenactors, so I've been doing that ever since I can remember. That's how I know Gaelic. When I was 12 I fell in with a group of friends who included John, the man I thought I would marry. But just six months ago — three weeks before our wedding — he left me for another woman."

At this, all the druids looked skeptical, blinking at her with wrinkled brows.

Ia butted in again, God bless her.

"If you waited that long to marry, then how did you expect to have enough children to guarantee the continuation of your line?"

Jaelle blinked herself back into the first century.

"Advances in medicine from now until my time are indescribable. We have machines—"

All the druids looked at her funny, and she realized she'd used an English word. The helmet could only do so much. Most of the time, there was a Pictish word or a Pictish phrase that was close enough, and it automatically translated for her so that she didn't even notice. But occasionally, she would say an English word, which almost always meant she'd mentioned something far too modern.

She thought about it for moment.

"A machine is something a blacksmith and a tinker make together that has moving parts and runs on something other than human power."

The druids looked at each other in wonder and then turned to her and nodded that she should go on.

"Anyway, advances in medicine from your time to my time are to the point where we can keep almost all infants alive, no matter what birth defect they have or how premature they are or whatever abuse was carried out on the mother."

She waited for Ia to say something, but unfortunately she didn't.

"So back when I was ... a young maiden, John and I were getting to know each other and I was sure we were going to get married. And we hung out with John's three brothers and his two uncles our age and all their girl-friends. I always thought I would know their children and we would be together always. But as soon as John's uncles turned 18 — on their birthday in fact, they're twins — they took off. Disappeared. Left their girlfriends 'high and dry,' as we say, without a word whether they were ever coming back or even if they were alive. The next day, John's twin brother also disappeared, and John's two older brothers, also twins."

Now Boanne did butt in, looking understandably skeptical.

"So many twins?"

Jaelle cleared her throat and looked around for some-thing to drink, found a pitcher and a mug, poured herself some water, then guzzled it down.

"Yeah, the druids wanted John's parents and his uncles's parents to have four sons, so they made them have twins. John stayed with me after the others left, and he told me what the deal was. One of his ancestors was tricked by a druid into selling his entire family into slav-ery. Every fourth-born son in his family must serve the druids, and John is the fourth-born son of his parents. All the rest of the guys left their girlfriends because they thought it was the loving thing to do, not letting them have children who would be slaves."

Jaelle choked up a little and brushed a tear from her eye.

"So anyway, the slavery that John has to perform for them is he finds hidden artifacts and returns them to my time so that they can use them. He's the one who gets sent to do their bidding, not me. This is his helmet, not mine."

Unwilling to see their reaction to this, she looked down at her lap so that she would be able to finish, then rushed on.

"I wasn't sent here by the druids of my time. I just found this helmet in John's things after he left me. I put it on, and here I was. Oh, and you should know that John's uncle's ex-girlfriend — Kelsey is her name — went to Celtic University in our time is also a Druid and can see into dreams and talks to me in my dreams when I'm here. She knows all about this and she knows all about you. But she would never hurt you. She's—"

The door burst open and Morna stormed in, hands on her hips and staring at Jaelle.

"Go ahead and hide in here all night. You aren't sleeping in Breth's room. You think you're special to him, but I'm more special to everybody here than you are. If I want something, it'll be done."

With that, Morna turned around and slammed the door behind her.

A few moments later, Jaelle heard the boards over-head creaking. Bile rose into her throat as she imagined the woman Breth had decided to marry making herself comfortable up there.

Continuing to whisper, she addressed Deoord.

"Has she slept up there with him?"

Deoord, Ia, and Boanne all shook their heads no, but they appeared to be thinking over what Morna had said.

The helmet had been on the table the whole time. Had Morna noticed it? Jaelle put it back in her bag and tucked that under her belt and then addressed all three of them, but mostly the two women. She figured they might understand.

"To me it was only a week I was gone, not two moon cycles like it was for you. And that's odd. Remember my friend Kelsey I told you about, the one who's a druid in my time?"

They all nodded.

"She and I communicated every night while I was here, so I know for certain time passed equally here and at home while I was here. It's only while I was home that more time passed here. The helmet has to be controlling that somehow, doesn't it?"

The three glanced at each other, then deferred to Ia.

For a moment, Ia reached for the helmet, but then she lowered her hands with a look of resignation.

"If I could read the runes inside, perhaps I could tell you. But as it is, I would only be guessing."

Hope bloomed in Jaelle's heart. She got the helmet

out, turned it so the light was shining inside, and stared at the curly pictures etched in the iron.

"My friend Kelsey can read Gaelic runes! I'll show them to her tonight when she visits my dreams, and tomorrow I'll tell you what the runes say. Do you know how to set it so that no time passes here while I'm gone? That's how her husband Tavish's ring works. He always arrives in the same spot, but no time passes while he's gone, so I know it's possible."

Deoord stood, looking determined.

"We don't know, but that doesn't mean none of the Druids from the other clans know. We'll go and talk to them about it. Sleep in here. I'll get you some bedding."

He rummaged in a chest and handed her some blankets, then glanced over toward an uncluttered corner of the floor. "It's probably best if you sleep in here. I'll tell everyone this room is not to be disturbed, but I won't say why, understand?"

Taking the blankets, she gave him a grateful smile. "Perfectly."

CHAPTER 8

Glad everyone had agreed to eat the morning meal elsewhere so that he could have some time to talk to Jaelle, Breth eagerly made his way up the spiraling stone steps between the broch's two thick outer stone walls to his father's private dining room on the fourth floor.

She was already awake when he opened the door, washing her face with the water from the drinking pitcher. She hadn't heard him come in, and he stood there amused while she finished.

A chuckle escaped his lips.

She jumped and turned, spilling the water all over the wooden floor, where it dripped between the planks. And then her eyes widened — most likely at seeing him wearing only his woad. He enjoyed her obvious attraction to him. She was almost salivating.

Well maybe she was just hungry.

"Shall I get you something to eat?"

She swallowed and put her hands on her hips, then sat down at the small round table where usually the chieftain's immediate family ate, along with the druids.

"Thank you, I'd appreciate that."

He quickly threw together a meal of leftover porridge and fried tubers, then brought over some of the berries the gatherers had brought in yesterday. Two tankards of ale from the keg on the counter completed the meal, and he put it all down and sat next to her.

Very pointedly, she bowed her head and was quiet for a few moments.

Sensing that he shouldn't disturb her, he waited.

When she looked up again, she wore a defiant look that reminded him of his days as a young man. It made him chuckle again.

She ate quickly without speaking, drank down the ale, then leaned back in her chair, visibly appraising him.

"I want to hear you tell Morna you aren't interested."

"Where is that coming from? Morna and I haven't been within spitting distance of each other since you arrived. Not even for a moment."

She looked up toward his room for a moment, then shook her head.

"You sure don't understand women very well, do you."

"What do you mean by that? I've been married. I know women pretty well by now."

With a faraway look in her eyes, Jaelle laughed.

"Morna harasses me every chance she gets."

And then she made her voice more high-pitched in a fair imitation of how Morna spoke, putting her hands on her hips as she wiggled haughtily in her chair.

"You will not sleep in his room. I have more influence here than you ever will, and if you think you'll get your way, you have another think coming. I'll get my way for sure. Count on it."

So that was why she'd slept here. But she was intoxicating. The way her eyes danced with anger dazzled him.

And then her face animated with anger as well, but that only made her prettier.

"And are you going to answer my question?"

He shook his head to clear it a little bit.

"I'm sorry, I didn't hear you ask a question. What was it?"

She growled a little. It was gorgeous.

"Are you going to tell Morna you're not interested in her, that you're with me and that's the way it's going to be and she should leave me alone?"

He sighed. He really didn't want to answer that question. She herself had yet to promise she was staying with him. And then he drew closer to her and put his arm around her and pulled her against him. Being close to her befuddled his mind, and he was guessing being close to him befuddled hers.

"I need a wife, it's true. And I want you to be my wife, that's also true."

He caressed her back and nuzzled his head against hers. He put his mouth next to her ear and spoke breathily, counting on making shivers go down her spine.

"Promise you'll stay here with me. That's what I need to hear."

She relaxed. At first, joy surged through him, but when she spoke, it was with sadness in her voice.

"I've been down that road before. John promised me we would be together the rest of our lives, and so I didn't need to make much of a life for myself. My life would be with him. So I got a job just to have something to do while he was away. A fun job that kept me amused, not a career that paid well. I didn't worry about supporting myself. I thought my future was secure with John's. How wrong could I possibly have been? So I'm not going to put my whole future in your hands until I've known you a while. I'm just not. I need to keep my job at the museum, at least for now. And that means I have to go back there. Tonight."

He didn't want to let her go, and so he didn't. He held onto her physically, caressing her and pouring all of his affection into her, hoping that would change her mind.

She let him.

Clinging on extra strong, he turned in his chair and kissed her as hard as he could, putting into it all his passion and desire, plus all the genuine respect he had for her — which he knew would turn into love in time, after they were married.

The two of them carried on that way for quite a while, but all good things must come to an end.

Besides, the clans had to move on today.

He pulled away first, sitting up straight in his chair and no longer leaning toward her.

"The clan moves on to the next broch today, so we can't sit here much longer. Only a few more moments. If we have anything else to say in private, we need to say it now. We won't get a chance again until tomorrow night."

Her face was troubled, but she didn't argue with him.

"I'm pretty sure each time-travel device is tied to one location, meaning the helmet will always deposit me at that spot in the woods where you first tripped over me. Tell me how to get to the other broch so I can find you when I come back next time."

He wanted to tell her. More than anything.

But his mother was right. A woman who wasn't willing to stay with him just didn't have what it took to be a clan chief's wife.

But if he told her that right now, she would leave right now. And she'd said she could stay until this evening. And if that was all the time he would ever have with her? Then he was going to enjoy it. He would tell her just before she left.

"It's too hard to explain sitting here in this room. We'll make it halfway there today, and then I'll explain from camp before you leave."

She looked doubtful yet hopeful as she gave him one quick peck on the lips.

"All right. What do we need to do before we leave?"

He gave her his most mischievous grin.

"Well, you need to go down to the sacred grove and get your woad on, of course."

The look on her face was comical and beautiful — and so Jaelle. He was glad he hadn't told her.

CHAPTER 9

Jaelle blinked to try and break the hold Breth had on her in his woaded glory, but it didn't work. He was stunning. More so because he didn't realize it. Branches of an oak tree swirled over his chest this time, waving whenever he moved his pectorals. The usual wolf pack covered his back, and as he turned to lead her down the carved stone staircase between the two outer walls of the broch, she was mesmerized by her view — around his sword — of the wolves leaping from rock to rock down the cliffs of his back and wagging their tails in the half-light provided by the sun peeking through the cracks between stones in the broch wall.

But Jaelle's mind was busy talking herself out of worrying. Why hadn't Kelsey appeared in her dreams? Was she all right? No, of course she was, and she'd been here before. She was probably just waiting a while to visit again. Feh. Just when having a druid friend would be convenient. Figures.

She and Breth passed into the main room at the bottom of the broch, and people turned to stare at Jaelle. Some of them were resigned to having her here — and she knew this was only because she was with Breth. Most of the people were regarding her with suspicion.

And who could blame him? She was a stranger, and so what if they thought she was in with the future Druids. And they doubtlessly all knew about Morna's arranged marriage to Breth. It was the way things were supposed to go, and Jaelle was gumming up the works, so to speak.

Well, she wasn't going to just grin and bear it. She was a fighter, and it was time she acted like one. She raised her head up high, pulled her shoulders back, and put on the calm competence of a warrior glancing at all the people.

And breathed a little easier when she saw that Breth was not oblivious to the reactions of the people — only to the effect he had on Morna. He noticed their stares, and he turned back toward Jaelle and raised an encouraging eyebrow.

Her heart melted a little more for him.

He searched her face with his kind blue eyes, made all the more captivating by the blue woad egrets which flew from brow to brow as he studied her.

"They will accept you once we're married. The sooner we are, the better. Come with us today to the next

JANE STAIN

broch. Don't go back to your time. I'm not going to beg you, though I will admit I want to."

How sweet! She felt her resistance weakening. It was on the tip of her tongue to agree with him. To say she would stay here and become his wife immediately in order to please all these people and gain their respect.

It was way too soon, though. What was she thinking? She could take the time. She'd go home for a day instead of a week. She'd beg Jan to give her a leave of absence. That was it. She needed a leave of absence from the museum. Jan could hire someone else to help out in the meantime. Six months' leave would be enough time to get to know Breth and decide whether or not to stay with him and become his wife. Yes, that was what she'd do.

And maybe the druids would still come up with a way for no time to pass while she was gone. They had all day.

But here Breth was right in front of her, blue eyes and all, and everyone was watching and waiting to see what she would say.

She put on her most flirtatious smile and swung her hips at him so that her skirt swayed playfully against his ankles. She locked her fingers together behind his neck — carefully so that she didn't disturb the woad.

When she spoke, she looked up into his eyes and beseeched them to see all the affection she had for him and all the hope she had for their future together.

"I am considering it. Very strongly. I want to stay with you."

She looked over her shoulder at all the people and lowered her voice to a whisper for only his ears.

"Deoord and Boanne and Ia are working on having the helmet bring me back here the instant I leave. Then my only concern will be getting from where it deposits me in the woods to wherever you are, so it's extra important that I be able to find the next broch. Are you certain you can't tell me now?"

For just a moment, she thought he took his deep breath because what he was about to tell her wasn't quite true. For just a moment. But then the genuine affection he had for her was back in his eyes, and he pulled her closer to him, staring at her and intensely radiating that affection as he spoke, pleading with her.

"You don't know what it was like for me. You had the helmet. You could come back any time you wanted. But me? Jaelle, I didn't know whether you lived or had breathed your last. I need a woman who's here with me every day, not just every month, every week, or even every other day. I have a clan to lead in battle. Someday, I will even be the planning chieftain of our clan. I cannot be wondering where my wife is and whether she will return to me. My mind needs to be unencumbered so that I can see how to defend us and provide for us without a nagging worry all the time. For the land's sake, Jaelle, stay with me. Be my wife."

If she answered him, it would be to say 'Not yet,' but her gut told her he would take that as a no. So she didn't answer. She held him and enjoyed his nearness, willing him to respect her need to go slowly.

As he turned toward the main door to leave the broch, he pulled her closer and whispered with a husky voice into her ear.

"Let's get on with this. I'm eager to watch you get decorated with the woad again. Such a treat."

She did her best to hold her head up and her shoulders back and walk like a warrior through the crowds of people she had never seen, but it was difficult when she knew she was blushing. A change of subject was definitely in order.

"How often are all the clans together like this?"

He squeezed her hand and swayed in his walk from side to side, playfully.

"This isn't all the clans, just those close enough to make it here to this sacred grove. There are many more in the far north, mostly along the shoreline, where brochs protect the land from the seagoing invaders."

Still clinging to him, she kept up this neutral conversation, lest he press her for an answer.

"Aye, I've seen maps in my day of all the brochs, and there are far more on the coastline to the north than down here by the wall. I guess no one told you the invaders were coming from the south across land."

As soon as she said it, she regretted it. What an offensive thing to say. She was trying to put him at ease, not challenge him.

But he didn't let go of her hand.

"Nay, the Druids always were telling us to make more brochs down here in the center of the land. I do think they knew. After all, they have time travel, so they probably did know. And now that we have proof of that in you, perhaps the chieftains with listen to them. You must admit, this being an island, defending the shoreline makes sense, aye?"

She squeezed his hand in apology.

"Aye, it does make sense, and I can tell you with assurance that far more raiders are coming, from—"

He returned her hand squeeze, pulling her around to gently put his mouth over her lips for a moment.

"Don't tell me. I don't want to know. I want to think I can make my own future, understand?"

She was yearning to deepen their kiss even after he had pulled away.

"I do understand. Must never tell you the future. But sometimes I may not be able to help myself. I will try, all right?"

He put his arm around her then, hugging her close as they walked, just like he had when she first arrived. Good.

She didn't want to risk her mouth saying anything else that might offend him, so she just looked around, drinking in the movements of his people, whom she did want to be her people. Unlike yesterday, they definitely were preparing to split apart and leave this place. All the children were herding animals now, as were many of the adults. They herded sheep and goats and cattle, enough to keep a thousand people fed. The children herded with sticks, and their dogs helped — the oddest looking sheep-dogs Jaelle had ever seen. In addition to children and herds of animals, there were adults pulling carts heaped full of bedding.

A man of about forty stopped in front of the two of them, wearing his woad determinedly, rather than joyfully. He nodded at Breth with respect, then turned a questioning look toward Jaelle.

This time, Breth didn't move on.

"Etharnan, I want you to know this is Jaelle, my love."

Whoa, his love! Had he really said that?

Etharnan held out his forearm. This was new. She looked at Breth to gauge his reaction.

He nodded the slightest toward Etharnan.

So she reached out her arm and they shook, much the same as business people shook hands in her time. But she noticed that while clutching sword arms, neither of them could reach their swords, not even with their left hands.

The fortyish Pict was speaking.

"I am honored to know she is your love, and I wish you much joy of each other."

Breth bowed his head to the man.

"I thank you."

And from then on, he introduced her in the same manner to everyone who stopped to talk.

Her heart swelled with hope, and yet she still didn't dare allow him to ask her again if she would stay beyond today, so she plied him with questions of her own on what was usually a safe topic, asking him about his work.

"Can you tell me what the meeting of the chieftains was about?"

When he didn't answer right away, she looked up at him, anxious that she might have committed a faux pas.

But his eyes held a faraway look that told her he was pensive about something other than her question, and when he saw her looking at him, he smiled at her reassuringly.

"Aye. A new chieftain has come up out of nowhere, swearing he will unite the clans whether we like it or not. He's given us a week to join him, or he says he'll take us by force. I say he and his ragtag crew are no better than the barbarians, and we should have nothing to do with him. But other chieftains are buying into the load of dung he has to sell."

Ah, asking about work had been a good move. Breth was back to his normal enthusiasm. She encouraged it as best she could, showing interest in her face as she rushed to keep up with his suddenly longer strides.

"I take it this is something new, the idea of all the clans joining up?"

He gave her a little side hug, as if to claim her.

"Yes. And I was on the fence about it at first. However, Father made me see that the larger a clan gets, the fewer folk have a say in what the leader decides, until almost everyone is out of the leadership circle. He's right, and I plan to stand by him and resist this Drest."

Breth's parents came up from behind and joined them.

Jaelle felt her knees shake a tiny bit.

But Breth's dad was charming, in an ancient-world kind of way.

"You don't know how glad I am you came back to us, Jaelle. Breth here has been missing you something awful."

Breth actually blushed a little! It was fun to see him treated as a younger man. This was a side of him she hadn't seen before, and she was enjoying it.

He regained his composure soon enough and shook his head teasingly at his father.

"I imagine you'd miss Mother if she were gone for two moon cycles too, eh?"

Breth's arm around Jaelle's waist was more firm and snug, and his hand caressed her hip with a tenderness that she would never have guessed he possessed, fierce warrior that he was.

But when she turned to look at him, she saw a face conflicted. He was enjoying this repartee with his father, but it made him sad. Why?

CHAPTER 10

Amid all the people scurrying this way and that with preparations for the long trek ahead to the next broch, Jaelle was still headed to the sacred grove to get her woad on. She turned to Almba with a question in her eyes. Why did joking with his father make Breth sad?

But Jaelle found Breth's mother staring at her accusingly, and with the hurt of betrayal. 'How could you put our son through such misery?' her look said. 'You should know better, you inconsiderate woman.'

Jaelle couldn't take the heat of that stare. She had to turn away, warrior or not. And then she wondered. She looked at the woman's husband for reassurance as she spoke, and got it.

"Almba, in your younger days, were you a warrior too?"

At his encouraging nod, Jaelle snuck a look at his wife.

Aw, that had been a good question to ask. The older woman's face softened considerably, and she threw her shoulders back and held her chin up in the warrior's stance, proud and with a different kind of fierceness once again.

"Aye, of course I was. One of the best."

She and her husband shared a look that said they were remembering years of fighting together, defending each other's backs and consoling each other through losses. He caressed her face — which of course was unadorned with the woad, seeing as how they were both past the age of fighting.

From her warrior stance, Almba started to appraise Jaelle as a warrior — and stopped short. Instead of the testiness that had been on her face before, the older and wiser version of the warrior acknowledged the younger and stronger version with grudging admiration.

This all took place in a few glances.

Breth's mother gave Jaelle a grudging nod.

"Aye, I think you know I was. I daresay I wasn't as good as you."

Apparently, that was all the older woman was willing to give. As soon as she had said it, she turned away and walked on in front of them, more quickly than she needed to.

Her husband rushed on to join her, turning back with

TIME OF THE PICTS

a warm apology on his face, a look that said, 'Don't worry, she likes you. She'll come around. Just give it time.'

But when Jaelle turned to Breth for reassurance, he was still looking at his mother, and his unschooled face told a different story.

This brought back the memory of Jaelle's last day living with her own parents.

🐚

MOM AND DAD HAD BEEN DRINKING AS USUAL, AND also as usual, you could hear their fight throughout the whole house, probably even out in the street. But the subject of their fight took a new turn this time.

"She's a grown-up now. She can go live on her own and stop mooching off us."

"She has a job, let's just charge her rent. Keep her here until she gets married—"

"With that no-good boyfriend she has? She'll be here the rest of her life while he gallivants all over the world with that fair of his family's—"

"Well if you want her gone, you go throw her out."

But Jaelle wasn't going to give them enough time to get around to that. She'd dealt with her drunken parents all her life, so she would show herself the door. She was 18 today, and she hadn't gotten so much as a "Happy birthday." And now this.

There were still three months of high school to get

through, but her plans to move out had just been moved up.

As usual, her parents were holed up in their bedroom, where they thought their drinking was a secret. Ha.

It was really simple to stick a chair under their doorknob while she packed up all her things — which fit in one suitcase. Then she removed the chair and ran through the front door with her phone out, calling her friend Amber to see if her parents would let her stay over for a few months.

Blood might be thicker than water, but what use was that anyway? The tears streaming down her face were definitely water, and they felt far more real than any connection through her blood.

JAELLE GAVE BRETH AN APPRECIATIVE GLANCE — this time not because of the delicious splendor of his naked flesh displayed through the woad clay decorations. No, this time she appreciated his stalwart confidence.

Breth's parents were tougher than most, being the chieftains of their entire clan. He was only the battle chieftain, under their thumbs most of the time. It had to chafe at him, yet he handled them with finesse.

Seeing her looking at him so, he turned more toward her as they walked to the Grove.

"I see you're happy here."

She pursed her lips to keep from smiling, but it didn't quite work. Her grin burst out.

Why did he have to be so darned confident in himself? It was sexier than all the cologne and fancy clothes and fancy cars – heck, even all the money — modern men flashed around to impress women.

Since the smile had broken out anyway, she put on her own brand of self-confidence and turned it around on him.

"It appears you're happy with me as well."

For some reason, this brought out a look of extra determination on his face.

"I could be, if you stayed here."

This again?

"I want to stay with you. I do. We've been over this. It's too soon—"

He threw his arm around her waist as they walked, pulling her as close to him as he could without smudging the woad designs. It was close enough. She could feel her resolve weakening with even this much body contact.

He let out a deep warm chuckle. It sounded like he knew being close to him befuddled her a bit. As he spoke, he nuzzled different parts of her with his chin.

"Aye, we have been over this, and all of me wants you to stay, needs you to stay. It's urgent that you stay."

He stopped them in the pathway and gently put his hands on both of her upper arms, waiting for her to gaze up into his blue eyes.

When she did, she saw yearning...

The last eyes she had known to hold such desperate need were her own, the night John told her he was leaving, that after ten years with her, he had fallen in love with another woman.

§.

JAELLE WAS COOKING, SOMETHING SHE ONLY DID once in a while. She lived on frozen meals most of the time, now that she was grown. When she was a child looking after her drunken parents, she'd had to feed herself more often than not, so she didn't enjoy being in the kitchen.

Lifting up the can she had holding her grandma's cookbook open, she peered at the recipe one more time. Half a cup of flour. She measured it out carefully the way she'd been taught in school, using a knife to level the excess off the top of the measuring cup back into the bag.

And then she stood there holding it.

What do I do with this?

Back to the cookbook.

Gradually add flour to the drippings in the pan while stirring until gravy forms.

The gravy just forms?

Going to the stove, she smelled the fat starting to burn.

Darn it.

She grabbed the pan handle. She meant to just scoot

the pan off the heat, but there were pots in the way: her potatoes and her green beans and her pudding.

How did other women manage to do this all the time?

There was a loud knock on the door of the tiny apartment she'd given notice on a week ago.

She was still holding the pan of drippings when she opened the door and John came in, storm clouds in his eyes.

"Put that down. We need to talk. Let's sit down at the table."

Before she could answer, he was storming into the kitchen, nothing but disgust on his face for the mess she was making.

How dare he?

"I'm finally cooking, and all you can do is complain?"

His 'Sorry' was correct, but not sincere.

Seeing red and giving herself a minute to collect her thoughts, she set the pan on the table and turned the burners off.

But when she saw him sitting there, she remembered what she saw in such a fussy man. Although small, he was wiry. His compact body was in the best shape it possibly could be. Hours of swordplay every day will do that. And although he was upset with her, he still looked her in the eye with the respect she deserved, something most men didn't think women needed.

And then she remembered how she must look and ducked behind the fridge to wipe the sweat off her forehead with a dish towel and use the toaster like a mirror while she brushed flour out of her hair.

When she approached the table, John didn't stand up like a courtly man. No, he looked her in the eye and nodded the slightest at her approach. It was a subtle thing that non-fighters might not recognize.

She appreciated it and did the same, but the back of her mind was troubled. It was going to be an epic fight, eh? One worthy of the warrior's acknowledgment?

Okay. I'm up to it. This time, I'm ready for your arguments.

And then as it was wont to do, her mouth spouted off her arguments before he even made his, losing any advantage having prepared them might have given her.

"It was you who wanted me to cook, you know. I'm just fine with frozen dinners. And where have you been? You were supposed to be here an hour ago."

Her hands had found their way to her hips all on their own as well.

I look like a shrew. One of my only advantages over him is my looks. Smile, Jaelle.

When she looked up into his eyes though, she saw that it wasn't working this time.

His look was hard.

"The wedding's off, Jaelle. There's still time to cancel the caterer, right? We have three weeks, and he said two. We'll lose the money for the hall and the decorations, but there's still time to cancel the honeymoon trip and time to tell everybody to cancel their plane tickets if we start right now. Come on, let's get this done."

&

BRETH'S EYES WERE LOOKING AT HERS THE SAME WAY hers had looked at John's that night.

Pleading.

Nearly begging her to stay.

CHAPTER 11

Plenty of people and a whole flock of goats passed in front of him on the path to the sacred grove without incident, but Breth was annoyed when his appeal to Jaelle was interrupted by Morna.

Approaching with two of the other clan chieftains, Brude and Leo, she swaggered up to Breth in the headstrong way of a leader who wasn't a fighter: head held high and shoulders back, never breaking eye contact, no caution, no hesitation.

He had to hand it to her; she'd come a long way from the shy little girl she once was, hiding behind her brother all the time at clan gatherings. But what did she want right now? He turned to her and the chieftains impatiently, with a question in his eyes.

She didn't make him wait. With command in her voice, she used the power trick of speaking just to him, as though Jaelle were someplace far off, not standing right next to him.

"She doesn't need to go down to the sacred grove. The druids brought her here, so she should be doing their work, not the work of a warrior. I've come to take her with me over to the supply carts, where she can be of help translating the names of the foreign goods the clans are willing to trade with us, seeing how she's such a language wizard. Leo and Brude here agree with me and have come along to help me escort her over there."

For the land's sake, Morna had gotten good at suggestion. If this were about anyone other than Jaelle, he might have agreed, just to encourage and reward Morna for developing this skill so well.

But no. If he had any hope of Jaelle staying, he needed to stand with her against all challengers.

Putting on his own air of command, Breth put his arm around Jaelle and stood firm, refusing to step up and meet Morna and her entourage. He felt Jaelle relax against him with relief, and he squeezed her gently with reassurance, though he couldn't do too much or he would smear his woad and anger the druids.

And instead of addressing Morna, he looked up and addressed the men. Two could play this game of pretending someone wasn't there.

"Is it true you don't think a warrior should be prepared, Brude? Leo? Deoord has already given her the woad on two occasions. She wore it well and did our clan proud defending against the invader Marcus and his minions. What would be the reason for denying her the pleasure of helping to defend us on our trip to Broch Seven?"

Visibly rattled by his speaking over her head, Morna glared at Breth with something that wasn't quite hatred — she couldn't afford to show him that, seeing as how she hoped he would be her husband. Her shoulders shook a bit and she stood there with her hands on her hips in order to look as big as she could, which wasn't very big at all. She was trying, though. Good for her.

Brude stepped forward around her, a wizened old planning chieftain now. The man had been formidable in Breth's youth, fighting off his share of Gaels. He'd thrown a spear farther than anyone else and had taught Breth how to throw one the way he did.

He gave Breth the warrior's nod.

"Not all the druids say she was sent to us by them, Breth. The people murmur that she's just another invader, a spy sent to us—"

Morna glowered with smugness at this revelation.

"Yes, and she cannot be trusted, so she should just help us with the trade carts, not go near the sacred grove. In fact, we should take her sword from her. It's not safe to have an armed stranger amongst us, now is it?"

This had to stop.

Right now.

Breth took Jaelle by the hand and turned on his heel, resolutely walked her toward the Grove, only speaking over his shoulder at Brude and Leo, right over Morna's head. Again.

"As I said, Deoord has already gifted Jaelle with the woad twice, and she did us proud. She's accompanying my clan, not any of the others. You are welcome to do as you will, but we will have Jaelle as one of our warriors on our journey. Good day and safe travels."

He half expected Morna to follow him and chasten his back, but she didn't. She'd grown smarter, as well as better at command. It made him smile.

Once they were out of earshot, he spoke to Jaelle from the corner of his mouth, still scanning ahead for signs that anyone saw Morna following them. So far, so good.

"We simply must be married as soon as possible. That's the only way to stop all these musings about how you're here as a spy and not loyal to the clans. It's highly unusual that we've waited this long to marry. Deoord can perform the ceremony as soon as we get to the sacred grove."

But Jaelle's face was closed to him, and she fingered the helmet stuck in her belt in its sack. She wasn't going to comply. He was going to lose her.

When she spoke, her voice was a little choked up. Good, she might still change her mind and stay. He would have to work on her.

"Sorry, Breth. Marriage is not something to rush into. I do want to marry you, and I'm going to find a way to be here without interruption for six months, getting to know you and your family and your ways. That's all I ask, and I don't think it's too much to ask. Six months is a short engagement where I come from. If you respect me, then you'll grant this request."

They were stepping into the grove now.

Deoord, Ia, and Boanne nodded at Jaelle in greeting as she approached them, but then shook their heads no in answer to some unasked question she had.

Surprising him, she disrobed matter-of-factly this time, with her head held high like the warrior she was. Doing him proud, she stood there nonplussed as they decorated her with the woad, even smiling at him a time or two and giving him a wink once!

It made his desire for her swell, and he just about salivated as he watched the druids paint dragons on her back, on her legs, and on her chest, their fire breathing up her breasts and under her chin. She was a spectacular work of art.

She did deserve her request. His parents would never grant it, but he wanted her radiant for this last day together, so he said nothing.

Once she was decorated, she took his hand and they walked together toward where the clan gathered for their walk to their next home.

As was typical of her, Morna hadn't given up. This trait would serve her well as a clan chieftain's wife and co-leader, but it was darn inconvenient at the moment. She strutted over to them with two new clan chieftains, Ru and Cal.

As before, the two men were old planning chieftains, past their prime, past warriorhood. Which only meant they had more authority than Breth did at these multi-clan gatherings.

As before, Morna made sure she led the charge, but this time her hands were carefully by her sides and she maintained her poise and attractiveness, looking at Breth flirtatiously as she spoke to the other men. This befitted the wife of a clan chieftain, darn her artfulness.

"Here she is. Let's take her over to guard the carts. You're right, Breth my dear. No sense letting a warrior go to waste. She's all decorated up and ready, so she'll be a good asset to the wagon train."

Morna was flouncing over with her arm out to take him in a half embrace right there in front of Jaelle when the first volley of arrows came down around their heads.

CHAPTER 12

Even as she drew her sword to fight off whoever had shot those arrows, Jaelle fumed. Every other moment, Morna stormed over and demanded to have things her way. The little brat needed a good spanking.

But the sight of Breth ordering Morna away brought a smile to Jaelle's lips clear through her anger. This was the second time he had come to her social defense today, and hadn't he been great, telling those other chieftains to have a nice day? Ha!

Jaelle's feet took her toward the cover of the trees, but also in the direction of the battle she could hear beating over the hill outside the grove as her head boiled with conflicting thoughts.

What an absolute gentleman Breth had been, telling those chieftains to mind their own business and let his clan mind theirs. He was third-in-command of the whole clan after his father and mother, and he had told those other chieftains what was what. For her.

She hoped the enemy would find her huge grin frightening rather than weak.

The first enemy out of a seemingly endless horde of Gaels in billowy knee-length dresses — both men and women — could be seen running up behind Morna.

As of yet oblivious to the threat, the woman Breth's mother wanted him to marry was sneering at Jaelle. 'Ha ha, he ran off without you,' Morna's look said even as the Gaelic man raised his sword at her back.

Without a second thought, Jaelle lowered her weapon at Morna's attacker as she ran, causing him to dodge away.

And saving the other woman's life.

There was no indication Morna was aware of the peril she'd been in, let alone who had rescued her. In fact, she sneered all the harder as she crawled under a bush and then skittered away like the little rat she was.

Even as Jaelle watched this show of contempt aimed at her, she didn't at all regret the instinct that had caused her to act.

Why don't I regret saving her? It would have been so easy. I could have just let the man get Morna. It wouldn't have been my fault. No one would have blamed me. Not even Morna.

No, she didn't regret her impulse to defend Morna. In fact, as Jaelle ducked behind a tree and jabbed to keep the Gael away, she felt happy. Because of her, the other woman had escaped into the bushes and would live out this day.

But I hate her, don't I?

The Gael jabbed back from the other side of the tree, and using a move borrowed from aikido, Jaelle subtly leaned to the side so that his sword missed her.

I do hate her. So why did I save her? And why am I glad to have done it?

While the Gael was off balance, Jaelle got her own jab in, and hit, and moved on toward the battle.

She still hadn't killed anyone, but she was awfully glad to have a blade in her hands. A way to defend herself and others. And then her mind started arguing with her. If Morna had known what Jaelle did, would Morna even thank her?

Jaelle blinked the thought away. Getting a thank-you wasn't the point. She knew that much.

Looking around for Breth, Jaelle took on the next enemy.

And the next.

Her best defense was to stay amongst the thick trees where only one person could come at her at once, so she didn't seek the higher ground where she might have an overview of the battle. It had to be huge force that could take on a thousand Picts.

And the Gaels had to have come up the river. It was the only unguarded approach. This fact niggled at the back of her mind while she fought one warrior after another, growing more and more tired and more and more determined not to succumb to exhaustion.

She was still proud of herself that she hadn't killed any of them, had but cut them so they wouldn't be able to fight anymore this day. However, she knew that sooner or later she would have to kill if she stayed here.

CHAPTER 13

Sure that Jaelle was right behind him, Breth fought for the high ground immediately, needing to see just how big the battle was. He made it to the top of the hill and peered through the rocks — and saw a swath of Gaels. They were overrunning the ten clans, there were so many Gaels.

He fought his way down the hill, still sure that Jaelle was close behind him. She wouldn't dive for cover the way the non-fighting women were trained to do at the first sign of trouble. He cut down first one Gael —a woman on his right— and then another —a man on his left— as they straggled up toward the sacred grove.

Jaelle should be at my side by now. Did she fall?

He looked up the hill he had just fought his way down. The way was clear, and so he ran back up there. Looking down into the thick trees, he didn't see her. She wasn't coming up here.

Should I go after her?

No, no. Warrior's Code: Don't get separated in battle, but if you do, then stay separate. Don't lose your head trying to rejoin your partner.

She would be all right, or she wouldn't. It would be foolish for him to try and do anything about it right now.

It seemed like it took him forever to turn back. He ran over the hill and began his way down into the broch valley where all ten clans were fighting for their lives, save for the few who may have made it into the broch. Everyone would have an honorable death at least.

The gatherers huddled in the middle of the carts where they had been trading, visibly losing hope at being defended from the outside and just waiting until they were taken over. Determined to save them or die trying, he ran.

And then out of the cloudy Highland sky, Drest's strange sword reflected a stray ray of sunlight as he led his band of renegades in a mad charge from the field to the left of the broch. With a loud whoop and holler, they crashed into the backs of the Gaels who had surrounded the carts.

For a few moments, all Breth could hear was the ringing of swords and spears and shields.

Drest had even more fighters than the Gaels did. With one clash from his forces, the tide of the battle had turned. Now the Gaels were the ones being overrun and outnumbered.

Breth hacked and slashed his way down over the next

hour, but he didn't even make it to the carts before he saw the last of the standing Gaels. The battle was over. The vast majority of the Gaels were running back over the hill and down to the river and away. If they'd had tails, they would be between their legs, they were running away so fast.

Drest may have been brash and crude and presumptive, but he was quite the battle commander. The ability to command so many ragtag men with no clan loyalty was a feat that in Breth's memory no other had accomplished.

Every year a few single men left the clan, dissatisfied with the leadership and wanting to run things their own way. Most were never heard of again, but some came back when they were old, begging their way into the clan's protection. Some even succeeded at this, and Breth had heard the stories they told. Without exception, life on their own hadn't been as they'd imagined, but they'd been too stubborn to come back until they couldn't manage on their own.

And Drest commanded a thousand such men who were yet young. Incredible.

Brude, Leo, Ru, and Cal had all made their way over to Drest and were patting him on the back and then shaking forearms with him — pledging themselves and their clans under his protection.

Before long, those surrounding the small brown man with the odd sword had taken up a group cheer usually saved for drunken nights around the Beltane bonfire.

"Rrr rrr rrr rrr!"

A spontaneous party was breaking out, complete with musicians playing and people dancing and hugging each other. Morna had rejoined the gatherers, who had opened up the carts and were tossing bags of rations to Drest's men, some of whom had already been to the broch and carried out kegs of ale.

Breth couldn't shake off the awe that had overtaken him on seeing the Gaels dispatched so quickly. He'd never seen them run away so scared.

The fighter celebration was in full force by the time Breth arrived. Even Father was there. He caught Father's eye, and a look passed between them.

"I know I said we should maintain our independence," said Father's look, "howsoever, you saw what happened here. We're in a vice grip. We have the invaders from the south on one side and the Gaels on the other. We need this alliance. I was wrong. We're going to backup Drest. We'll join with him."

"Are you sure?" Breth asked Father with his own look. "We can still leave, move on to the next broch." Breth looked over his shoulder toward Broch Seven, where they'd been headed.

"No," Father said with not only his eyes, but also with the firm line of his lips pressed together and the squareness of his shoulders in the Warrior's stance. "I can admit I was wrong. I can't keep on the wrong path once I've seen the right way to go, and we're making a turn here."

Breth held up his hands in the oldest sign of

surrender known to man. He smiled a grim smile at Father and shrugged a little in acquiescence.

"You are the clan chief. I defer to you."

Drest and his top ragtag men had been hoisted up on the shoulders of men who were still loyal to their clans. Men who had deserted were being lifted up as heroes. Perhaps just one mistake didn't mean a man's life was over and irredeemable. Perhaps they were now on the right path, helping.

Breth met Father's eyes again and nodded in the direction of their saviors.

Father nodded and gestured.

"Yes, we should go over and join in on the back patting and the general festivities."

So they did. And before long, everyone was relaxing around a huge bonfire topped with the clothes of fallen Gaels — who had been conscripted as slaves, very few being dead.

Drest got up on top of a mound of rocks that his men had assembled for his small stature. He stood up there turning around and around slowly, waiting for everyone to quiet down so they could hear him. Finally, when only the flapping of the flames in the wind competed with his voice, he spoke.

"We will be staying here and fortifying the area. It is the best place from which to stage raids on the wall. We will leave the broch's roof un-thatched against future fire attacks, and we will all be safer because of our great numbers."

The cheers started low, but then twenty more people joined in and thirty others until gradually it became a call of war that could doubtless be heard by their retreating enemies.

Breth looked around for Jaelle, but he didn't see her.

CHAPTER 14

Jaelle didn't see Breth anywhere amid all the fighting, but she did recognize three female woaded warriors from his clan. She had spent time training them in modern sword fighting techniques, and they had trekked together out to the cave.

They made her part of their defensive circle now in the sacred grove, all back-to-back. But oddly, the Gaels were just running by now. Running by in droves. For a bit, the women watched anxiously, prepared to battle any Gaels that turned on them. But when none did, they began a tense back-to-back conversation.

"Have you seen Breth?" she asked them as her eyes scanned the Gaels running by in their flowy dresses.

"Aye, he went down the hill toward the cart staging area."

"Is that far?"

"It's too far to go right now, Jaelle. Maybe later..."

Jaelle knew the woman was just being nice. It didn't appear there would be a later. The Gaels kept running by, probably to surround them, and even here in the forest where cover was adequate, there were too many Gaels for the Picts to last long. She wished she had Breth here to spend her final moments with, but his clanswomen would have to do.

"It is been my honor to fight by you."

"Jaelle, you honor us by being here. And we would stand with you as our new clan chieftain's wife."

"Aye. You bring as much to the table as she does. More, even."

"I can't let this go untold. I wasn't really sent by the Druids. I just found the helmet in my ... unfaithful man's left behind things."

"We knew that."

"You did?"

"Aye, we did."

"How?"

"We just... Come on, why would druids send a warrior back? They keep to themselves. If they were to send anyone back, it would be another druid."

"Rumor has it they do send other druids back, and it's never a good thing for the clan that gets a visit."

"Aye, 'tis often quite a bad thing indeed."

"Please tell. I can't die without hearing about this."

"It's just rumors and whispers, you know."

"I know, but those are often true, right?"

"Well, this is unseen in our lifetime, and if the Druids

have seen it, they aren't telling the rest of us. It's rumored the druids from the future send druids back for their own selfish reasons, not to help the rest of us."

"Oh, tell her the real stories. Don't beat around the bush."

At this, they all laughed, because they had all just been beating at Gaels around bushes.

"These Druids when they come, they always come in white robes. They're looking for ordinary things that have special properties — such as your helmet."

"The druids welcome them as if they are traveling from another country, just passing through."

"They say you'll know the visitor druid is from the future by his or her complete inability to survive alone."

"Jaelle, you are not like that at all."

"Aye, you've taught us skills way beyond our imagining with the sword and the spear and the dagger."

"Aye, you are one of us."

Oddly, the barrage of Gaels had stopped.

All four women stood there looking at each other for a few moments, and then Jaelle turned to rush up the hill.

Ione stopped her with a hand on the wrist.

"You don't know what you may find over the top of that hill. The Gaels may have taken over down there."

Jaelle calmly waited for the woman to let go of her wrist.

"That may be, but if I don't find Breth, I don't really care."

Ione let go of Jaelle's wrist just as Jaelle caressed the bag with the helmet.

Doreen nodded toward the bag.

"Get it out then, and be ready to use it."

Jaelle did so, but just before she turned to run with the helmet in her hands, all three women hugged her.

Common sense took over when Jaelle neared the top and made her slow down and go down. As she crested the hill she was on her belly, peeking through the low-lying branches of the bushes and camouflaged, she knew, by her woad. It was a much more sensible way to see what was going on down there. Who knew, if their arrows were trained this way, she might die before she put on the helmet, which she now got out again.

She inched the last of the way up on her belly, anxious to see Breth still standing.

And she gasped.

Oh, Breth was fine. He was sitting on one of the carts with Morna. Had his arm around her amid all her gatherer lady friends toasting and making merry.

But that wasn't why Jaelle gasped.

Off to the side amid his own little gang of partiers stood John, special sword strapped to his back and laughing with a load of Picts she hadn't seen before, who were obviously his entourage.

What should I do?

It got even worse, because John's new woman came over and put her arm around him and he squeezed her lasciviously, right there in front of all the rest of the people, who cheered him on.

They started to chant the name he had taken for this time.

"Drest! Drest! Drest!"

Jaelle started lowering the helmet down onto her head.

But then she saw John hand something to two of his Picts, who turned right toward her — no, toward the way to the river.

She still wanted to leave, but dread loaded her stomach. She just knew something was terribly wrong.

CHAPTER 15

Breth was looking around for Jaelle when Morna crept up beside him and put her hand on his. He was so taken off guard that he didn't shake her off. And anyway, what was the harm. They were all but promised to each other. No one could talk any more than they already were.

The look in Morna's eyes was relief.

It made his heart ache. Her clan had been eliminated by the barbarians two months ago. It was no wonder she wanted all the clans united, fearing what might happen to her new clan as well.

He put his arm around her shoulders and gave her a hug of reassurance.

"Don't worry. We're going to stay here all joined together against both sets of invaders. Drest is right. We have a huge force here. We'd be foolish to break up. There is strength in numbers after all. I thought we would be stronger apart, but I'm coming around to the idea that we're stronger together."

Yes, he'd been right to reassure her.

She relaxed against him and put her head on his shoulder.

"I'm so glad to hear that. You know how hard it's been, losing my clan. My brother is all I have left, aside from you and Talorac and your parents. You're the closest ones to me now."

CHAPTER 16

Jaelle's three woaded women warrior friends were headed toward the carts like everyone else, but John's two Picts were going toward the river. Maybe they were getting water? But no, they didn't have anything with them to carry it, not beyond their own water skins for their personal use. Where could they be going?

Jaelle held her breath as they passed by her — and for a good few seconds afterward as well for good measure — then followed them as quietly as she could. Which didn't need to be too quiet, because the two were talking.

"That went better than I thought it would."

The other man laughed.

"You're telling me. I had no idea it would happen so quickly."

"Yeah, I thought we would be here all day."

"Did you see the looks on their faces?"

They laughed again.

"Aye, they sure were glad see us!"

"I could get used to this."

"I know. Feels good to be appreciated, doesn't it?"

"Aye, it does."

"Do you think they'll all join up?"

"Yeah, I do."

"Seeing the tables turn on them will be reward enough."

"Well I don't know if I should mention it or not, but he promised me more than just that."

"He did?"

"Yeah."

"Glad to hear it. I got offered more too, but I wasn't going to say anything in case you didn't get the same offer. You never know."

"You're right about that. I should've kept my mouth shut."

"No harm done."

They had come to the river, which they crossed in the shallow part where the women had bathed the last time Jaelle was down here. Once they were across and up the opposite bank and had started down the other side of the hill, Jaelle followed again, slowly so as not to make any splashing noises. The water was cold now, and she had to bite her teeth together so they didn't chatter.

Anywhere else, I'd be glad to be in a river in September, but here in Scotland? Bbbrrrr.

She did miss some of the conversation while she was

in the river, but after she'd crept up to the top of the bank and peered over, she saw them down in the trees and made her way into the woods closer so that she could hear what was being said. She hadn't gone a dozen steps when she froze.

She heard four voices. Speaking Gaelic.

Unlike Pictish, which was a lost language in the 21st century, she knew Gaelic without the helmet, so she could hear how different it was now from the 16th century version she had learned from John's grandfather at the Renaissance Faire.

And then a branch moved and she could see four men in the woods: two wearing Pictish short trousers and two wearing Gaelic leine tunics.

Each Gael held a small drawstring pouch that clinked when he tossed it from hand to hand. Simultaneously, they each peered into their bag and counted the coins until visibly satisfied, they smiled at the two Picts.

It would all have been confusing if she hadn't understood what they were saying to each other.

"I really like the touch where you ran in from the other field," said one of the Gaels. "Made it clear you were not part of the gathered clans but someone coming in to save them from elsewhere."

"Yes," said the other Gael, "and we appreciate that you came quickly, before too many of us fell to their swords."

One of the rebel Picts raised his head in tribute to the fallen.

"You didn't lose anyone dear, did you?"

The first Gael shook his head no.

"Nay, we always put the troublemakers on the front line. They took the brunt of your people's attack before you got here. We had some indication from which direction you'd be coming, so we put the ne'er-do-wells on that line. Rest assured our forces are still intact enough to help you fight the barbarians."

The second Pict shook forearms with both Gaels and turned back toward the river.

"Glad to hear it. See you soon."

"See you soon," both Gaels called out just before they turned and disappeared into the darkness beneath the trees.

Jaelle crept back into the trees herself just in time for the rebel Picts to pass by her on their way back to the party, whose cheers and general merrymaking could be heard even from all the way over here.

CHAPTER 17

The same three women warriors ran up to meet Jaelle as she got near the carts, where everyone had gathered to drink ale and generally party.

"We'll go with you, Jaelle."

"Yeah, we'll help you tell him what's what."

"He can't treat you like this."

"And you are going to marry him, not her."

Touched by their loyalty but sure it wouldn't help, Jaelle gestured for them to follow her.

"Yeah, come with me, but I have something much more important to tell him."

"What is it?"

"I don't have the energy to tell it more than once, so come along and I'll tell everybody at the same time. It's a good thing they're all gathered."

But when Breth saw her coming, he jumped up out

of Morna's embrace and ran to meet Jaelle.

How weird. If he thinks I'm staying a minute longer than it takes to tell him Drest is John and John's a traitor—

Not even giving Jaelle the opportunity to say anything, Breth grabbed her and kissed her passionately, putting his whole body into it and making her knees weak. They fell into one of the carts, and people heaped covers up on top of them.

"Looks like you two need to be alone."

Peals of laughter.

An angry Morna growled.

Jaelle gave herself a pep talk as she lay there in the cart with Breth, gearing up to tell him the shocking news. But he kept her mouth busy with his.

After this kiss, I'll tell him.

No, after the next kiss.

What was I going to tell him?

Before long enough though, outside hands were digging at the covers and voices were asking for their attention.

"Breth, you're needed."

"There's a chieftains' meeting."

"They say we're all staying here and not going on to the other brochs."

"They told us to send you right away."

Jaelle grabbed Breth's hand as he got out of the cart.

He turned, and seeing her face, he waited for her to get out and took her along.

Good. A chieftains' meeting would be an even better place to tell everyone what she knew. Looking down, she saw that both her and Breth's woad was smeared. And she was still naked. She didn't care. The chieftains needed to act in unison and boot John out of their camp. Out of their lives.

They were rushing her and Breth over to the bonfire...

And then she saw John. He was the center of this meeting, holding forth like a king at court. She couldn't tell everyone in front of him. Worse, she knew that as soon as John saw her eyes, he would know that she knew he had paid the Gaels to attack in order to gain these people's alliance. He would see her holding Breth's hand and know where her loyalty lay.

And this was not the John she had known and loved. No. There was a hard set to his jaw, and his eyes were ruthless. What would this new John do to Breth's clan if he saw that she knew his secret scheming ways?

She took the helmet out with her other hand while they walked and then tugged on Breth's hand until he stopped and turned to her.

She kissed him again while she raised the helmet over her head, then backed away so Breth saw what she was doing.

"Meet me in the woods where you tripped over me as soon as you can get there."

She looked pleadingly into his eyes as she put the helmet on.

CHAPTER 18

Breth gave out a cry of anguish even as his feet carried him over to the chieftains' gathering as fast as they could move, using up as much of his energy as they could so as not to leave him any with which to hurt someone.

How could she just leave like that? Didn't she... But no. How would she possibly know he meant for this to be his and her last day together? He hadn't told her.

She'd been radiant in her woad. The taste of her was still on his lips. He groaned and growled and made fists as he ran, but the distance was too short to get all that out, and he knew his face still showed pain and hurt when he arrived.

Father came over and put a hand on Breth's back. It was meant to reassure, Breth knew, but it didn't work.

"I saw her put the helmet on. Quite a few people did.

If you look around, you can see that she made an impression on us."

Breth turned back toward the carts. Back toward the revelry at the bonfire. It was high noon now, and for the midday meal, the gatherers were passing out rations that had that been meant for the children, gatherers, and elders on the journey. And yes, everyone was visibly talking about Jaelle, woaded warriors and craftsmen in those baggy Pictish shorts alike. The two types didn't usually mingle like this, but she had made such an impression that they were all gathered together in groups.

Breth was shaking when he turned back to Father.

"So I just forget her?"

Father massaged Breth's shoulder a bit, then turned him toward Drest and the other chieftains, who were politely waiting for his attention.

"No one's asking you to forget her. We are only asking you to move on. Embrace your duty to the people."

The people? Breth questioned Father with his eyes.

But Father pointedly turned to Drest and gave the intruding chieftain his undivided attention.

Drest didn't have a very loud voice, but he had a trick for booming it out that intruded on Breth's thoughts.

"We are all staying here, all ten clans, plus we'll gather more. I know many of you have heard, but just to make no mistake, I wanted to tell you personally. This location is ideal for sending raids to the wall. And we must prevent that wall from being completed. I have seen the future, and I know this wall will be the end of the people's will, the end of life as we know it. The end won't come right away. It will take a few hundred years. But this wall, these invaders from Rome, they are the beginning of the end. It just gets worse from here. More southern invaders will gradually take over from the Romans, but they will all have a hatred for the people north of the wall. Eventually they will send everyone out of these lands so that they can raise sheep. Sheep! Is that what you want for the hundredth children of your children's children?"

The reaction of the chieftains was immediate. Most of them rallied to Drest, going over to pat his back and shake his forearm and declare their support.

Breth was ready to stand with Father for their clan's independence, but Father went over to Drest as well and shook the odd little brown man's forearm. And declared their clan's allegiance. At first, Breth looked on with puzzlement and outrage. Why had Father changed his tune so drastically after convincing Breth the clan needed their independence?

But then Breth found he just didn't care.

"I'm going to look for her. Give me until the woad wears out."

Father didn't even hear him. He was spellbound by the strange chieftain.

Fine. Breth headed off in the direction of the woods where he had tripped over Jaelle.

Talorac found him a hundred steps later.

"Go get her."

Breth gave his brother a grateful smile.

"Thank you. I tried to tell Father where I was going, but..."

"Aye, the talk of Father's change of mind is almost as great is the talk of Jaelle disappearing."

Breth laughed a tiny bit as he climbed the hill that would take him out of the broch valley. The hill he'd seen her coming down yesterday, the vision that had filled him with joy.

CHAPTER 19

Jaelle saw the world spin when she put the helmet on. She would just go to the bathroom first. Oh, and while she had a mirror, she could tidy up the smeared woad a bit. Hm, and maybe wash under her arms. And then she would put the helmet back on and meet Breth in the woods.

Would he be upset with her for leaving so abruptly?

Probably, until she explained about Drest being John and paying the Gaels to attack and her not wanting Drest to see her lest he knew she was onto him. Once Breth knew all that, he would understand why she'd left.

She could still feel his lips and his body against hers, and it made her throb with the need for more of him. Soon, she promised herself, soon.

Her living room came into focus, and she turned to make her way up the hall, taking the helmet off as she did so, preparing to set it down on the bathroom counter.

But someone grabbed the helmet!

Whipping around to attack them, she saw that it was Richard. And that she would never be fast enough with her attack.

He was already putting the helmet on, and he gave her a triumphant look as he disappeared with his face still five inches from her fist.

Jaelle screamed and then cried, beating her fists against the wall.

"No! No, no, no!"

She ran back into the living room and cast about for her phone. Kelsey would know what to do.

But her friend didn't answer.

"Kelsey, where have you been? I expected you in my dreams last night. There's this modern druid named Richard who puts up exhibits at the museum and he had a stone from the time of Hadrian's Wall with a picture of John on it, and anyway, he stole the helmet! I need to go back and tell Breth about John paying the Gaels to attack—"

The second beep cut her off.

She called Kelsey again, and again she got voice mail.

"I can't stand just sitting here alone not talking to someone about this, so I'm going to call Amber. We'll do a conference call and try to add you every few minutes. Please answer."

Come on, Amber, you'd better answer.

Jaelle's hand shook as she found her friend in her contacts.

Come on. Come on.

But Amber didn't answer either.

"Amber, what in the world is going on? I can't reach Kelsey, and that's bad enough, but I thought you would answer my call no matter what! Richard stole the helmet and John is paying Gaels to attack Breth's clans! I didn't get a chance to tell him! I'm so glad you updated the other MacGregor ex-girlfriends right now. I'll try Lauren. But get Tomas to get Tavish to have Kelsey contact me as soon as possible!"

After only two rings, Lauren picked up. She'd been the girlfriend of John's twin during their faire days, so she and Jaelle had been close, but they hadn't spoken since Lauren got dumped seven years ago. John had insisted, and now Jaelle felt stupid for listening to him.

"Jaelle?"

"Lauren, it's awful. John is there posing as some Pictish warrior named Drest and he's organized the Gaels against the Picts and he's pretending to be on Breth's side and he's got them fighting each other and it's horrible."

All choked up, Jaelle had to stop for a moment.

Lauren sounded confused.

"Why are you talking to me? Go back there and stop him!"

Now Jaelle was crying. Sobbing so hard she could just barely choke out the words.

"A stupid Druid named Richard from my work stole the helmet just now right out of my hand! He put it on and he's there and I'm stuck here without it. I keep calling Kelsey and she doesn't answer. Neither does Amber. Where the heck are they?"

"We don't know, only that they won't be reachable for a while. Tavish and Tomas, too. Something super-secret is going on."

"Great, just great. What am I going to do?"

"Well, you're in love with this Pict Breth, and you want to go back to his time and marry him and live happily ever after, right?"

Jaelle opened her mouth to say she wasn't sure yet, that it was too soon, but she realized it wasn't true.

"Yes, I do want to go back and marry him right now, waiting time be damned."

"That's the spirit. We could call Vange, tell her what her son's doing and see if she'll help us. If John has a time travel device, then certainly Vange and Peadar will have one too and can take you back there."

Jaelle sighed heavily.

"No, it doesn't work that way. Each device only goes to a certain place and time, and anymore, the Druids arrange the settings, not the time traveler themselves. And John was the only one going to Breth's time. He did talk to me a little bit before he met the woman he left me for. No, if anyone is going to be able to help, it's Kelsey. I'll try adding her to our call."

Jaelle waited what seemed like forever but was probably only 30 seconds. And got voice mail yet again.

"Hi Kelsey. Please call me!" She hung up and said to Lauren, "I really don't see why she can't just answer her phone. She's only doing archaeological work. It's not like she's attending royalty."

"Maybe she is. Maybe she's back in time attending a queen or something, and that's why she can't answer her phone."

"No, she and Tavish are lucky enough to have their time-travel device set so that they return the moment they left."

"Well, it couldn't hurt to call Vange, could it?"

"That's looking like our best option right now, and I don't know for sure that she can't help, just that it's unlikely. Sec, her number's in my phone book, but not in my phone."

Jaelle looked around frantically for the book she and John had compiled together, half of her not wanting to find it. Because then she'd have to look at his handwriting.

And while she did so, her mouth spouted exactly what she was thinking.

"Lauren, I'm so sorry I didn't call you sooner. It sounds like you forgive me already, but I want you to have my heartfelt apology anyway. John said I shouldn't talk to you or I might give away the secret, and I was an idiot to listen to him. Thank you so much for taking my call. You didn't have to, and I wouldn't blame you if you hadn't. But I can't imagine what I'd do without you. I'm about to go crazy with you—"

There was a loud knock on Jaelle's front door.

Jaelle just pretended she wasn't home. She didn't

want to deal with her nosy neighbor right now. No one else ever came and knocked on her door except for Mr. Jones, the grocer who lived next door and sometimes came over ostensibly to offer her day-old milk, but she knew it was really to see what was going on here in her house where there used to be a man living and all of a sudden there was a woman living.

Whoever was there knocked loudly again.

"Aren't you answering it?"

"No, I don't think I can deal with it right now."

But then a voice she knew but couldn't quite place came in through the crack next to her front door.

"Jaelle, I ken ye are in there.. I ha come tae help ye."

Puzzled and a little bit curious, Jaelle went to a window in her L-shaped house that looked out on the front porch from the side. Barely parting the blinds, she peeked out.

And instantly jumped back. It was that grey-haired archaeologist from the museum, the one who had tried to get her into his car. Alasdair! Who had told him where she lived? Had he followed her bus? Despite her training as a warrior, her heart thumped in her chest.

Lauren sounded worried, too.

"What's going on, Jaelle?"

Before she had a chance to answer, Alasdair came over to her window. This time, he spoke very softly.

"Jaelle, Kelsey sent me here tae help ye. Been trying, but I canna if ye willna hae it."

"Did you hear that?" Jaelle whispered.

"Did you mention Kelsey to him?"

"No."

"Is there any way he would know about Kelsey from phone conversations you had that he might have over-heard or something?"

Jaelle wracked her brain, but she really didn't think so, not unless he had been on the bus with her. She raised her voice at the window.

"All right, I'm going to let you in, but know that I'm on the phone with a friend who knows where I live." Under her breath, Jaelle gave Lauren her address, then raised her voice to the window once more. "Understand?"

"Good. Aye, I ken. I'm glad ye hae friends involved. That's good. Good for ye. I'm going o'er tae the front door nae, and I wull leave my hands oot sae ye see them. I mean ye nae harm. Kelsey begged me to come here and help ye, and that's what I hae been trying tae dae."

But tough warrior though she may be, Jaelle was not willing to welcome in this creepy old man in just her woad.

"Be right back," she called out as she dashed to her bedroom and pulled on jeans and a T-shirt. When she got back to the front door, she opened it quickly, stepping to the side in case he tried to rush her.

But he didn't. Alasdair was just standing there with his gnarled old hands out where she could see them, as he had said.

"May I come in?"

Jaelle jumped a little.

"Yes, I'm sorry, do come in and sit down. Shall I get you some water?"

Alasdair smiled at her kindly this time. Had his creepiness been her imagination? No. No, it definitely had not been. He still raised the hairs on her neck, even with the kind smile on his face – and she was sure he meant the kind smile.

"Nae, but I dae thank ye."

He sat down on her couch, the couch she and John had picked out together what seemed like a lifetime ago. John had turned out to be such an evil... He needed to be stopped, and all of her queasiness and reservations needed to be set aside if Alasdair had really been sent by Kelsey to help her. All she needed to do was confirm that he had been.

"So, how can you help?"

Holding her gaze with his and moving very slowly across the room, Alasdair raised up his hand and opened it palm-up to reveal a small flame that was emanating from his hand.

"Whoa."

"What?" asked Lauren breathlessly.

Still holding Alasdair's gaze, Jaelle trained her phone's camera on his hand.

"Watch this."

With a slightly amused look on his face, Alasdair did his little parlor trick again.

Lauren echoed Jaelle.

"Whoa."

Alasdair crossed his ankle over his thigh and relaxed into her couch, putting his arm up on the back.

"Sae ye see, we Celtic University professors took Kelsey's plea for help seriously, back when ye were stranded at the Roman fort."

Jaelle got excited at this. She'd forgotten how Kelsey had promised to send her help, and he had magic! Maybe he could time travel! Maybe he could get her back to Breth! But she tried her best to temper her glee. What was the catch? Kelsey's druids didn't exactly have the best reputation among her group of friends, seeing how they controlled John, John's uncle Tavish, and John's grandfather Dall. And would control every fourth-born son in their family.

"I understand you Druids don't just go around helping people like superheroes, so what's your interest in this?"

The grey old professor gave Jaelle a slight nod and a knowing look.

"It's true. We only help if yer need fits into our agenda, but it sae happens that stopping Richard meets all o' our agendas."

Jaelle gave Alasdair an appraising look.

"Stopping Richard. Not helping Breth and his people, but stopping Richard."

Alasdair nodded.

She tried her best to seem intelligently puzzled rather than mystified.

"Stopping Richard from doing what?"

CHAPTER 20

Even as Breth moved on toward the woods where he first tripped over Jaelle, he wondered why he was headed that way. She was just going to leave again, and seeing her for a few more hours would only hurt his heart.

But he found that he couldn't stop himself from going to her.

She had looked so desperate staring into his eyes, had pleaded for him to meet her, some deep concerning need plainly showing on her face. What could it possibly be? Why had she felt the need to put the helmet on so suddenly?

Perhaps that was why he couldn't keep himself from walking out there to meet her. Perhaps he was so full of bafflement that...

No. No, he knew that wasn't it. He also knew that whenever she asked him to meet her, he would go. It made him feel weak, in a way, but even as a warrior, he found that he didn't mind. He wasn't ashamed. He was nothing but consumed by the need to see her again.

Will I ever be able to move on? After she leaves tonight — saying she'll be back in a few days but really meaning she'll be back in a few months? And if I do go through the motions of marrying Morna, will I truly be a husband to her?

I think not. I think my heart is irreversibly given to someone who...

Breth, control yourself. You don't know Jaelle is toying with you. Meet her and find out what's so urgently needed, and then make up your mind about what to do next.

Yes, that was the best plan of action, so he made his way to the woods where he had first met the love of his life. And he waited there — not patiently, but at least with a hopeful heart.

He waited while the short shadows of midday made it through the trees and elongated into the long shadows of afternoon and finally became the darkness of evening. He sat up all night awake, waiting.

Because of the woad, he didn't feel hunger, nor the need to sleep.

He did need water, however, and he hadn't brought any. Should he go to the river?

No, what if she came while he was gone? Besides, he hadn't been doing anything but sitting here. He would be fine for a little while longer without water, so feeling a bit lightheaded, he waited. And waited.

Finally, when he had but an hour of magic sustenance left — and it wasn't strong, seeing how he and Jaelle had smeared the woad — Breth reluctantly turned back home.

CHAPTER 21

J aelle held out the glass of water Alasdair had requested, despite his prior protest saying he didn't need any.

He eagerly held out his hand for it.

"Thank ye. Now there are a number o' relics linked tae specific places, and the helmet is just one—"

His lecture lasted quite a while, and she could tell it was something he had presented many times. That was odd, seeing how Kelsey hadn't ever heard about time-travel objects while at his university. She'd had to fend for herself when confronted with them. Hm.

Finally, he came to a stopping point.

"However, the key is the link between the item, an era, and a location. This link can be copied."

Jaelle was about to explode, so as soon as there was a lull in his talk, she cut in.

"But the helmet is gone. Can you make another way

to time travel with whatever you have in that pouch of yours? And what does any of this have to do with stopping Richard? You still haven't told me what he's up to."

The professor sat back on the couch with his water and took a long drink, pointedly waiting for her to calm down.

She made herself relax back into the couch as well and put one leg over the other, resting her hands at her sides.

The creepy old guy smiled slightly.

"All right, I wull cut tae the chase, as ye young folk like tae say. I can make a way for ye tae return tae yer lover if ye are willing tae trust me."

Lauren piped up.

"How do we know we can?"

Plainly hearing her, he got up and headed toward the door.

"I reckon ye dinna."

Jaelle jumped up and took his hand.

"Please. Please, I'm willing to give anything a try. Please stay."

CHAPTER 22

Talorac came out to greet Breth as soon as he topped the hill over the broch valley. He looked around and then back to Breth in sadness.

"Where is she?"

Breth shook his head, unable to say her name, let alone that she hadn't met him.

His brother put his arm around him and gave Breth's upper arm a squeeze in obvious sympathy. As this was unspoken, Breth was able to take it without breaking down, which was doubtless Tal's intent, being a warrior as well and understanding.

Tal spoke offhandedly.

"A new druid has come into the fold. He has an odd name. Richard, he calls himself. Not sure if I'm saying that right, but I think that's what it is. Anyway, he introduced himself to Drest and says he's with the druids down the wall a ways, the ones that don't want any clan — I know you've heard of them, aye?"

Glad to have something else to talk about, Breth threw himself into this new conversation.

"Aye, that group Deoord sometimes goes to for counsel and instruction, so he says."

"Aye, the same. Anyway, Richard says they're behind him. He presented their support to Drest 'in order to ensure that you truly defeat the barbarians from that place they call Rome'."

Breth gave Tal his 'Are you sure?' look.

"What assurance do we have that he actually does have the support of the other Druids and isn't just some imposter looking for information to pass on to the Romans, as he calls them?"

Tal gave Breth his 'Oh yeah, I'm sure' look.

"This Richard has a sickle that Deoord assures us belongs to the head Druid from that very same clutch of them. We're all convinced."

"Well, given the power of those Druids, it's a good arrangement, isn't it?"

Tal nodded.

"A few of the chieftains disagree—"

"Let me guess who."

Tal laughed.

"No need. But Drest is officially over all ten clans now. All the chieftains pledged to him last night while you were gone, and he accepted Richard's help willingly."

They were getting near the broch now, and people started to greet them.

"Grand news, eh?"

"Here's to being rid of the barbarians!"

Nodding to each greeter and exchanging pleasantries, Breth found his thoughts wandering again to Jaelle. Why hadn't she come? Was she well?

No, don't think about it. Think about the battles ahead and the alliances that are forming and this new druid Richard and you might be right in the head. Keep your mind off her, for your own sanity.

But one greeter asked a disturbing question.

"What did you think of the strange look Richard had on his face right after he shook forearms with Drest, as if he'd seen a vision or something?"

&.

THE CHIEFTAINS' MEETING HAD RESUMED TODAY. Drest was once again standing on his stone, presiding. Apparently, he was taking suggestions as to how they would begin their long series of raids on the wall.

Resigned to his clan being part of a larger ten-clan group, Breth presented his own ideas.

"We tried taking the fort quietly in partner pairs before. It would have worked if we hadn't been so careless. I think we should try that again and take over the fort closest to this broch and stage further raids from there."

Drest nodded to Breth in thanks.

"I like this idea. We shall begin as soon as we can gear up, so get to that. Dismissed."

❧

THE RAID ON THE ROMAN FORT WAS A SUCCESS. Breth even managed to save Drest a few times, and Drest saved him a few times. It would have been a glorious day but for two things.

One, why hadn't Jaelle come back? Every time he crossed the courtyard of the fort, he saw her there kneeling in the center, Nechtan swinging the bag and hitting her in the head, and her disappearing from him. It haunted him so bad that he almost fell a few times.

He had been the one who suggested they all stay here. Even now, runners were headed up to the broch to bring back a few necessities. But not everyone was coming here. The fort wasn't big enough, and while the broch wasn't either, it wasn't so near the enemy. Two clans would stay, the two most loyal to Drest: Brude's clan, and Leo's.

Maybe they'll keep Morna here with them, since she sees eye to eye with them.

What? Wherever had that thought come from? Of course Morna was to stay with his clan. What was he thinking?

Well it would be nice if she would leave awhile so I didn't have to decide quite yet.

Haunted. That's what he was.

The second reason it wasn't a glorious day was because Breth had the uneasy feeling someone was watching them from the bushes up the hill, where he himself had hidden to watch the fort. One time, he thought he caught sight of a white Druid robe, just one time. It was probably his imagination, probably. But he still felt uneasy, and he kept looking up there until an hour before sunset, when his clan and the seven others who were going back to the broch were ready and Leo and Brude's clans were settled in.

Breth thought the walk back to the broch would be a relief, but it wasn't. He still had the itching feeling that he was being watched.

CHAPTER 23

To Jaelle's immense relief, Alasdair stopped walking toward the door and turned back toward the couch. She gave him her friend-liest smile when he turned to look at her.

"Why did Richard have to take my helmet, anyway? Couldn't he just check something out from the University?"

Alasdair shook his head.

"He canna. Richard has been expelled from his professorship. If ye like, ye can go online and check that fact, since I can see ye still dinna fully believe Kelsey sent me."

Lauren piped up.

"Let's try her again. She's got to answer her phone sometime. I know she and Tavish just got married, but seriously."

Plainly able to hear Lauren on the phone through Jaelle's earbuds, Alasdair smiled sadly.

"Kelsey willna be answering her phone until at least tomorrow."

Jaelle waited for an explanation, but when he didn't say anything, she gestured her frustration.

"After that announcement, you have to tell us why."

Alasdair nonchalantly sat down on the couch once again, his arms on the back, his ankle crossed over his thigh, and his foot wiggling.

"I canna tell ye. Jaelle, if Richard has yer helmet — and I hae no doubt what ye tell me is true — then he has gone back there, and he is verra dangerous. With enough ley line energy, the man believes he can become immortal. A great place tae dae that would be in Scotland under the right combination o stars, but he needs tae sacrifice a hero, wuth yer Breth being the obvious choice."

With Lauren on the phone, Jaelle felt a bit of reassurance. What Alasdair said was so far-fetched, but... She could call Vange, but it had been true, what she said about time travel objects only going to certain places and times and not being resettable by people. John had explained that himself, once upon a time.

She looked at Alasdair intently.

"Am I being recruited officially to help stop this Richard person? Is that why John left the helmet here?"

Alasdair gave her the smallest of smiles.

"All I can tell ye is that John didna leave that helmet

here. If I try tae tell ye a thing more, I am blockit, unable tae even speak."

They sat there for quite a while, studying the looks on each other's faces. Jaelle thought Alasdair looked sincere. And determined.

Alasdair gave her his sternest gaze.

"Ye be willing tae let me get ye back tae the time o the Picts?"

Jaelle raised her chin and sat as a warrior, resolute and ready.

"Yes."

He nodded the slightest.

"Hae ye nothing suitable tae wear?"

She went to her closet and got out the dress she had made while cooling her heels that week she had to work for the museum. It wasn't complicated, just a simple knee-length sheath dress with a slit up the back so that she could move easily — but it was hand-stitched and made from homespun linen, which had cost her half a week's wages. Unfortunately, she didn't have any suitable shoes. Oh well.

He looked impressed when she came out.

"Verra well, come closer. Sit right next tae me sae our sides touch."

While his mere presence had raised the hairs in the nape of her neck, sitting next to him like this made her shake and quiver involuntarily.

If he noticed, he didn't say anything, just took her hand in his. It wasn't a gentle hand hold, the kind a friend or lover would give you. No. It was... It was as if he held the control lever on some sort of machine.

Disturbed, Jaelle drew her hand away.

He let go immediately.

"This has tae be a voluntary thing on yer part, Jaelle, or I willna dae it."

She still was shaking and trembling, quavering with the creepy vibes that came off him. Nevertheless, she was going through with this. She would get back to Breth.

"I am in this voluntarily, it's just that... My instincts are telling me I shouldn't."

He nodded.

"Ye hae good instincts."

He just left it at that, and they sat there in silence, the only sound her grandmother's clock, ticking away on the mantle.

She gave his side a nudge with her elbow.

"Well?"

Alasdair chuckled, a good-natured chuckle.

"Ye hae spunk."

And then, his presence was inside her mind. Just how much of her thoughts could he see? Her memories?

"I could," said his voice inside her mind, disembodied. "But it would be an evil thing for me to do, and if I can help it, I don't like to do evil things."

If he could help it! When wouldn't he be able to help it? What have I gotten myself into?

Jaelle's instincts told her to wake up now, snap out of this trance she was in so that Alasdair could connect to her thoughts. But no. She needed to get back to Breth. This was going to help, she knew it was. Somehow, she knew the druid was sincere about that. He meant to get her back to see Breth. She knew he did have ulterior motives concerning Richard, but he would get her back to Breth.

Richard was another story. She did not trust him at all, and she be glad to help stop him, whatever he was trying to do.

She didn't see Alasdair here in her dream state the way she saw Kelsey in a dream, walking around and floating them up on top of staircases and through walls as if they were in a movie. No, with Alasdair it was more like he was another presence right there in her very mind. It wasn't visual at all, but of course she still knew he was here.

She could not read his thoughts at all, though. She only heard what he deliberately said to her.

He had been keeping silent while she ruminated and got used to him being here, but now his little thought bubble inside her head spoke up again.

"We all have obligations outside our control, or that we've agreed on. I say this by way of explaining why there are sometimes circumstances where I can't help the evil practice of reading someone's thoughts against their will."

What? Obligations? What is he talking about?

Jaelle's instincts were kicking into high gear now, telling her she should snap out of it and get away from this lunatic before her sanity was at stake. A sense of panic pervaded her mind — except in the small corner where Alasdair's presence loomed. Oddly, that small corner of her mind was calm.

"Of course you have such obligations, Jaelle. You have an employer, after all. You can't tell me they never give you directions you don't wish to follow?"

Jaelle concentrated. Instead of thinking to herself, she deliberately answered Alasdair's question, directing a thought to him.

"It's not the same thing at all. I don't do anything evil at the museum's direction, just sell our souvenirs to the tourists by making suggestions along the way during the tour. It's distasteful, sure, but it isn't evil."

Alasdair's little corner of her mind was still calm.

"Isn't it? Through your power of suggestion, you cause them to spend money they didn't intend on spending."

Jaelle could feel the warrior instincts kicking in. Alasdair was attacking her, maybe only on the psychological level, but attacking nonetheless. And so her instincts shifted from 'run away' to 'turn and face your attacker. Keep your eye on him.' It occurred to her that perhaps this was his intent.

He seemed amused at this last thought.

"No, I was just answering your question. I find that if I answer all the objections raised to my presence in a mind, the mind calms itself, and we can get to the business at hand."

"Oh."

"Is it working?"

"Yes, I suppose it is. Discussing it with you like this is much more comfortable than wondering why you're here. I guess I'm getting used to it. I suppose that's a good thing, and yes I would like to get to the business at hand."

"Very well then, picture the helmet in your mind. Remember all the details you can — inside and out."

"That's easy," she thought to him, doing as he asked. "I spent a lot of time studying it to show Kelsey, hoping she could tell me what the runes inside say. Hey, can you? Here are the runes inside."

"I can read the runes, but I cannot tell you what they say. I am restricted by the same sort of directives your employer gives you, but whereas you are selling things to tourists, I am teaching things to people — or not. Understand?"

"Yes. I'm surprised to, but I do understand."

"Good. All right, keep that helmet in your mind as vividly as you can, and yes, turning it every which way helps immensely. Keep doing that. Concentrate on it. Also, if you can bring to mind how it feels on your head, how heavy it is, what it smells like, the sounds when things hit it. Give me the idea the helmet is on your head right now."

She did, but this took so much concentration that she forgot to speak with him in her mind and instead just had random thoughts again, vaguely aware that these were the type of thoughts that her mouth would go off with when she was awake.

How is this going to help? How long will it take? How much time has passed? An hour here is eight hours where Breth is!

"The connection between an item, an era, and a location can be copied. An item can also be copied, and if the dream walker is powerful enough, he can copy it from the image in your mind."

I need to wake up.

"Are we done?"

"Wake up, lass, and see for yerself."

She couldn't believe her eyes. She rubbed them just to make sure they were actually open and this wasn't a dream. She even did the old cliché thing and pinched herself, and then had to believe her eyes. Wow.

Alasdair was sitting next to her on the couch, and on his head was a perfect reproduction of John's helmet.

As usual, before she could form a coherent thought about a new discovery or surprise, her mouth spouted off about it, telling everyone in the room — which was just Alasdair — but also Lauren on the phone what she was thinking.

"You're gonna steal my idea of the helmet from me just like Richard and go off to Breth's time without me, aren't you?"

Looking much more warlike with the helmet on his head, even though his hair was gray and his face was wrinkled and his hands were gnarled, Alasdair shook his head no with sadness in his eyes as he sat there next to her on the couch.

"No, no I'm going tae take ye with me."

He put his hands on her upper arms and touched his forehead to hers through the helmet.

"Hold still. This is gae'na take concentration on my part."

It was such a relief to have him out of her mind and to have come to her own senses that she didn't mind at all this holding still and letting him do whatever it was he was doing.

"What's going on?" Lauren said in her ear.

"I'm not sure, but I'm okay."

"Well that's good at least."

"Hush, ye" said Alasdair. "This is difficult enough without ye distracting me with talking."

"What is he doing?" Lauren hissed in Jaelle's ear.

"I'm making a copy o the helmet for Jaelle tae wear. Now be quiet."

Feeling like a disobedient kid in school and kind of liking the sensation, Jaelle tapped the phone as surreptitiously as she could and turned it on video chat, training the camera on Alasdair in the helmet.

Lauren gasped, but to her credit she kept quiet.

Before long at all, Jaelle could feel a copy of the helmet forming around her own head. It felt exactly like the original, and if Alasdair's was any indication, it looked just like the original too. She was really going to get to go back and see Breth!

CHAPTER 24

Drest saw Ragan cringing as she lay naked on the hilltop hidden in the trees while he had sex with Ida. Well, that was just too bad for her. She hadn't been promised anything.

RAGAN FELT THE TEARS STREAMING DOWN HER FACE, felt her nose running, and didn't wipe her face. What did it matter what she looked like? No wonder Drest hadn't married her. He had no intention of being only with her. Not five hundred breaths ago, Drest had lain with Ragan, and she had thought Ida was only along to wait on them.

How foolish I've been, leaving my clan for this stranger.

He had seemed so exotic and different and interesting. Well, he was all of those things, but he was not much more. Drest was not half the man her father was, nor her brothers, nor any man in her clan, nor in these other clans. He was selfish and dishonorable.

I wish I were back home!

How pathetic and whiney she sounded. She took a deep breath, let it out, and finally wiped her stupid girlish tears away with the back of her hand.

You are a grown woman, Regan, not a mewling child.

Pushing her hurt feelings aside, she tried to think. What should she do? She was far away from her people, and she was not a warrior. There was no way she could make it home on her own.

When next she looked over and saw how ardent he was with this other woman, Regan had the urge to take Drest's knife out of his scabbard and plunge it first into his back and then into Ida's, warrior or not. It would serve them both right. Indeed, she was reaching for the knife when she heard many feet approaching.

She quickly dressed before the footsteps reached the top of the hill, smugly not pointing out their approach to Drest and Ida. Let the two of them be found naked and in the middle of their... pleasures.

It was a bunch of Gaels who came.

Ragan held Drest's knife in front of her defensively, looking through the trees for an avenue of escape that didn't take her past the skirted men. But they had surrounded her and Drest and Ida, who now gasped and would have screamed in fear if Drest hadn't put his hand over her mouth.

Foolish, foolish, foolish girl! You left your family, your whole clan, for this bag of scrum who is now going to get you killed!

Rather than be killed or worse by one of the Gaels, Ragan turned the knife the other way in her hand.

But one of the Gaels got to her before she was able to do herself in. He grabbed the knife away from her and gave her a look that said she was a foolish girl indeed. Far from harming her, he looked sympathetic, and aside from taking the knife away, he kept a respectful distance between them. She didn't speak his language, yet the two understood each other.

She gave the Gael a look and gestures that said 'Yes, I know I'm a foolish girl. Look what my man is doing with another woman. I would rather run off with you, quite frankly, than stay here a moment longer.' But that was not to be.

Drest pulled out of the, ahem, situation he was in and got to his feet, completely ignoring Ida, who was staring fearfully at the Gaels.

While Drest spoke to them in their Gaelic language, Ragan took Ida's clothes to her and helped her put them on, speaking softly to her.

"You're welcome to have him, if you still want him after this."

"Are you kidding?"

The two held each other, shaking with fear as they watched Drest with the Gaels, half expecting him to offer the two of them up as one would offer food at a gathering.

DREST FUMED AT THE GAELS. COULDN'T THEY SEE he was busy?

"You are na getting any more money from me. Now get oot o my sight."

"Are na we gang tae gae after the Romans together?"

Drest heaved a sigh.

"Aye, we are, howsoever, that time is far off. For now, leave. I wull send word when ye are needit."

IT WAS A NEAR THING, BUT THE GAELS LEFT without killing any of them. At least that was something for which Ragan could be thankful.

CHAPTER 25

Alasdair backed away and gave Jaelle a bolstering smile.

She smiled back, excited.

"Shall we go?"

But he looked significantly at her feet.

She followed his gaze down to them, looked back up at him, and angrily shook her head.

"You have a wayward druid to stop, and I have a mad warrior to stop, and you're worried about my footwear?"

He laughed. Again it was a good-natured laugh, but it was at her expense.

"I willna hae ye slowing me. Nae, dinna fash. There be a simple fix, but it wull involve ye lifting that dress up."

"What?" trilled Lauren.

Jaelle had been sure she could trust this man, but this

last comment raised more than just the hairs on the back of her neck. She pulled away.

But he was laughing again, that disarming good natured laugh.

"Nae for thon reason, ye ninny. Sae thon I can fix the woad and guarantee yer feet dinna get cut. Tae bad I didna ken ye lacked shoes afore I made the helmet, but we wull work aroond thon gaff."

Slowly, Jaelle relaxed again.

"You can do that? Fix the woad, I mean?"

He lowered his chin and raised his eyebrows, putting his hands on his hips in a look of mock indignation. For an old guy, he was quite the communicator.

Well I guess that makes sense, him being a professor and all.

He began in his lecturing tone, raising one eyebrow at her and turning his head slightly to the side.

"One doesna become a druid as auld as I am withoot thon I ken aw the tricks o' oor trade."

She put on a skeptical look of her own, calling his bluff. Hm, maybe his pride could be used to her advantage here.

"All the tricks of your trade? Time travel, dream walking, premonition, woad warrior armor, and ... ?"

His smile was meant to be sheepish, but she knew he was mocking her again. He was far too good a communicator, reading her intentions right into her words and body language.

"Now, now, Miss Penzag. Ye ken as a warrior that it

isna in my best interest tae reveal moves I hae na yet displayed. Nay, not even tae allies, for alliances dinna last."

She gulped and pointed her finger back and forth between the two of them.

"How long does this alliance last?"

He gestured for her to take off the dress. There was nothing lewd in the gesture at all, just a matter-of-fact look such as a tailor might wear when appraising how a garment looked on her – though she knew he was appraising the woad, not the dress.

Bare underneath except for the woad, she raised the dress up so it bunched under her chin, which she also raised in proud defiance. Even though she did feel slightly... okay, greatly, uncomfortable, she had said she would do anything to get back to Breth.

Because she already had a magic helmet on her head but had not yet been transported back to Breth's time, it was plain that Alasdair controlled his copy of the helmet. That made sense, and so she was at his mercy and figured she might as well get this done as quickly as possible.

To her surprise, rather than take out a pot of the woad clay and reapply it, Alasdair simply whet his fingers with his saliva and used the smeared woad already on her to touch up areas that weren't so smeared, until she had quite a few intact designs on her body.

The whole time he did this, his eyes were focused in deep concentration, which allowed her to study him.

Alasdair had clearly never been a warrior. He didn't

have the muscles. No, he had been a lecturer and a druid most of his adult life. He didn't get outside much. His face wasn't as wrinkled as she would've expected, based on how gnarled his hands were. Arthritis, she guessed.

His touch was just like Deoord's, artistic rather than — well, rather than the way a man normally touches a woman. And Alasdair was an artist. He made the dragons on her chest breathe fire even more realistically than Deoord had, and she could see them flying around on her body when she bent to look.

She waited until he was done to tell him so.

"Are you sure I need to wear the dress? It will be such a shame to cover up your artwork."

He smiled in thanks.

"We need tae hide yer presence from Richard, and from John. Wear the dress. Withoot it, ye wull stand oot tae much. Remember, twa whole days hae passed in their time while ye were here six hours. Nae one else wull be woaded. The men wull be in those baggy Pictish shorts they wear, and the women in dresses. I wager they still wag their tongues aboot ye disappearing when ye put the helmet on, sae ye dinna want tae stand oot, nay."

She sighed.

"Yes, I agree, my best course of action is not to let John know I'm there at all. Because I'm afraid the moment I look in his eyes, he'll know what I know. I need to tell Breth first and give him a chance to tell the others. I need to wait at least that long before John knows I'm there, and really I'd rather not talk to him at all."

He looked reassuring.

"I hae a hunch I wull ken a lot if I can manage tae but touch John's hand, sae aye, let us keep ye away from him until then. From yer memories, I ken the feel o John's presence, and sae I can help in that regard, if ye listen tae me."

Jaelle laughed.

"All right. Can we go now?"

The world spun, and in a few moments Jaelle was facing Alasdair in the place in the woods where Breth had tripped over her. She watched the old professor's helmet fade away and felt her own disintegrate as well.

CHAPTER 26

Breth was incredulous. Drest was good on the field of battle, but he had absolutely no idea what he was doing when it came to clan politics. He was pressing the chieftains way too hard, making them do every little thing his way.

The mood of the camp was like a stormy night compared to the glorious day of the bonfire celebration. All the people had cross looks on their faces, and although each person he encountered nodded at him, they didn't exchange greetings the way they normally would.

It was no wonder. For some stupid reason, Gede, Chieftain Ru's little son, had wandered into the middle of the chieftains' meeting and asked one of the chieftains the way to broch nine. That was something none of the people, not even a little child, would do unless someone

157

at least as important as a chieftain put them up to it. And who would do that?

Drest had been so unnecessarily angry about it though. He had nearly killed Ru over it. Things were getting out of control. If Breth hadn't stepped in and grabbed the boy and run with him, there was no telling what would have happened.

Even now, Breth didn't have any faith that things were going to turn out all right. He was headed toward the sacred grove, anxious to talk this over with Deoord and Ia and Boanne. They were wise. They would know what to do.

Breth was almost to the sacred grove when he saw...

"Jaelle!"

"Breth!"

He ran to her and she met him halfway, and the two of them clutched each other on the shady path to the sacred grove, almost at the very spot where Morna had mocked Jaelle with Brude and Leo, saying she should guard the carts.

But all thoughts of Morna fled his mind as he held Jaelle close to him and felt her holding on just as tight.

And then he saw that she was not alone. An old, old, old druid was with her. He had to be a Druid, because nobody else lived so long. The man was at least seventy. His gray hair was long and came over his shoulders, and his hands were more gnarled than any Breth had ever seen.

But Breth didn't care that the druid stood there,

waiting to be acknowledged. He kissed Jaelle with all the longing he had stored up the whole night he had waited for her.

And the stranger didn't interrupt.

After not long enough at all, Jaelle pulled away and started speaking. He tried to kiss her again. Whatever she was trying to say could wait. But she spoke through that, so this must be important.

For the land's sake, it had better be.

It was.

"Breth! Listen! Drest is from my time. I used to be... betrothed to him, and he paid the Gaels to attack so that he could rescue you and the other clans. You cannot trust him. I was going to meet you in the woods, I was! But another druid from my time, not this one, stole the helmet from me. I only just met Alasdair here, and so it took him quite a while to convince me to trust him enough to let him... put me into a trance so he could copy helmets for us. I don't have the helmet, so I'm not able to leave here—"

At this, Breth whirled with all the command presence he had in him to face down the old druid.

"If Jaelle wants to leave here, then you will make it possible."

The old man smiled at him and then wrinkled his nose in amusement. He spoke with the oddest accent ever. If Breth didn't know such a thing were impossible, he would have sworn it was a combination of Pictish and Gaelic.

"She doesna want tae leave here. She wants tae stay and get marrit tae ye this verra day. I saw it in her mind."

What!

Seeing red, Breth lunged at the man, druid or not.

"In her mind! If you have violated her trust—"

Breth felt Jaelle's hands on his waist from the back, trying to pull him away from the old man.

"I gave him my consent, Breth. Leave him be, please! It was the only way I had to get back to you. He's here to help. And he wants our help stopping the Richard druid who stole my helmet from..."

Breth had backed off, and Jaelle turned to Alasdair.

"Just what is it Richard wants to do?"

Richard! I knew that druid was trouble. This explains much - my feeling of being watched, Gede running into the chieftain meeting. He does need to be stopped, but it will take actual evidence for me to survive accusing a druid.

Alasdair gestured for the two of them to follow him over to the sacred grove, and without waiting to see if they did, he went that way.

Breth didn't find it at all odd that a druid knew the way to the sacred grove, figuring he must sense the place.

Breth hugged Jaelle by her waist and followed.

"So do you trust this Alasdair?"

"Aye, I do. He was in my mind and could have done any number of things and he didn't, and he's a professor at the university my good friend Kelsey attended. She trusted him enough to send him to help me when I called out to her in my dreams as a prisoner at the Roman fort."

Hm. Breth would give Alasdair the benefit of the doubt. For now.

CHAPTER 27

Still giddy about the messed up situation with the boy, Richard watched the goings on from the bushes. Just one more incident would send Drest's popularity spiraling down and put Richard's plan into action. The stars would align soon, and he would not miss his one chance, no, he wouldn't.

Staring at the man, Richard cast illusion.

Richard didn't feel any change, but a quick look down verified that his limbs were now brown and small. His eyes even looked out at the world from a lower height.

Satisfied, he looked away from Drest over on the other side of his clump of trees to a clearing where other people had gathered and were talking. Good, there was a likely woman for his escapade, one who was too young to be married yet and who was not high up in her clan status.

Keely was a beauty — green eyes, rosy red lips,

flaming red hair. This would be fun. Richard made his way over to her side as Drest, at first amused by the head bows.

"As you were. I just came over to visit."

Pointedly unsure he meant it, at first the people continued to pay him attention.

Tempted to just blast them all into oblivion, he nevertheless held his temper and made a show of gesturing benevolently for them to resume their conversations.

Finally, they did. He listened awhile, and every so often, he turned to Keely and asked her opinion on this or that, gradually showing appreciation at her answers. Still quite young, she was not yet confident in her charms as a woman. That was why he had chosen her, as with her, flattery would get him everywhere, he knew. Well, disguised as one so important as Drest, it would.

The others were deep into their discussions now. Good.

Time to make his move. He put a gleam in his eye and showed it to her.

"My, but you are beautiful."

Keely looked around just the slightest amount, but she kept her eyes mostly on Richard, well, on Drest. Good. She was interested.

When she spoke, her tone was flirtatious, if a bit worried.

"Where is Ragan? Aren't the two of you —"

Aw, how charming. She had ethics.

"No, she broke that off."

Her face turned to elation at that.

Casually and slowly, he turned and started strolling away from the gathering, not at all surprised when she rushed to his side.

"Tell me about your part in the defense against the Gael raid."

His hook was working itself deeper and deeper into her jaw. He could tell by the way she prattled on about how she wasn't a warrior but she had helped keep the children safe. She was earnest all the while, trying to sound impressive, bragging as best she could. Trying to impress him. Good.

They had walked far enough away that they wouldn't be heard, and he was confident no one would see them go into the bushes in the dark. He spotted a suitable location through there, a small clearing with a good covering of soft leaves and grass. He was going to enjoy this.

CHAPTER 28

Puzzled, Breth watched Keely beat on Drest's chest, crying and wailing.

"You said we would be together! How could you?"

Quite a few people were casting angry glances in Drest's direction, including Father. What a mess.

Breth went over to Father.

"What happened here? It can't be what it looks like, can it?"

Father's face was stormy.

"We made a mistake, that's what happened." Father lowered his voice. "There's a secret meeting tonight without Drest. Things are going to change."

Breth looked over to where Keely was now being consoled by her mother, Lavena, and if looks could kill, Lavena would have killed Drest three times over by now.

Breth wanted to go to them, but he knew this was women's business. He'd better stay out of it.

"Father, you don't know the half of it." And Breth quietly told Father what Jaelle had told him about seeing the Gaels take money from Drest's men.

Meanwhile, Chieftain Uist was trying to counsel Drest.

"Drest, you have to keep it under control. This kind of thing may have been overlooked in your travels, but it's not going to fly here."

But Drest angrily turned on Uist, one of his staunchest supporters.

"I didn't have anything to do with that woman! Yes, I take my share of bedfellows from the clan women, but I wouldn't go with one so young."

Uist raised up his hands and backed away.

"Just trying to help, but obviously you don't want any help, so..."

Breth went back to the sacred grove, frantic to find Jaelle and breathing much easier when he found her, sitting with Deoord. The two of them had their heads together, deep in discussion. He hated to interrupt, but...

"Jaelle, Jaelle."

She smiled a radiant smile when she looked up and saw him.

"We're talking about Alasdair's ability to recreate magic items from memories. Deoord thinks maybe Kelsey will be able to do that in forty years or so!"

Looking over at the druid for confirmation and

getting it -- interesting -- Breth walked over to Jaelle and gave her a hand up, took her in his arms for a long moment, and walked with her toward the secret meeting, which would be starting soon.

"That's wonderful. Listen, we have to go..."

She looked up at him with nothing but love and devotion in her eyes. Maybe Alasdair was right and she meant to marry him?

She squeezed his waist.

"Sure, of course."

The bonfire had already been started. All the leaders sat around it with their wives and children as if this were informal, and there was a distinct lack of a rock platform for Drest to stand upon.

Breth brought Jaelle and made his way over to Tal, who wasn't normally at these things.

"I hope someone's keeping Drest busy so he doesn't wander over here."

Tal looked off toward the hill out of the broch valley, where torches had been mounted on pikes in a circle.

Breth followed his gaze. Sure enough, the younger warriors were having a tournament, with Drest as judge.

CHAPTER 29

Jaelle clung as close as she could to Breth's side throughout the chieftains' meeting at the bonfire, caressing his arm with her hand and his knee with her knee... doing everything in her power to show him her love short of bringing up marriage right here in front of everyone. That needed to be a private matter between the two of them, that decision.

She had told the chieftains all about John's hiring the Gaels to attack so that he could rescue them, and the Picts were rethinking their commitment to John as Drest, their leader.

And then Richard showed up.

He appeared without warning, and Jaelle didn't have a chance to hide from him, but he winked at her in such a way that left little doubt he'd known she was here. He got into the center of the group.

She turned to Breth.

"Can he do that?"

Breth shrugged with one shoulder.

"Why not?"

She gave him an 'Are you crazy?' look.

He elaborated.

"Usually they all would come. All the druids in the area would present their unity of opinion. But druids come to these meetings all the time. They're our counselors."

Jaelle wasn't the only one who noticed just one druid had come to the meeting. She saw some of the chieftains whispering to their wives about it.

But Richard had the majority of their attention, and he was obviously enjoying that fact, striking scholarly poses in that aggravatingly presumptive way he had while he waited for them to quiet down before .

"So now you know, with the help of Jaelle here, that Drest is really John from her time. I truly believe John is attempting to help you keep your homeland throughout the next few centuries. However, if you continue to follow his lead, he will become king here, and his children after him. This would in turn destroy the culture of the clans. We do not advise you to follow him."

There was a general hubbub, mostly agreeing with Richard, but one chieftain spoke up.

"Regardless where he comes from, Drest is our chieftain. We have all sworn loyalty to him. We cannot revolt against him, for that too would destroy the culture of the clans."

Jaelle leaned into Breth and gave him a squeeze. She was enjoying this. That comment had put Richard in his place. He couldn't just waltz in here and single-handedly determine the way things were run, no more than John could.

Breth squeezed back, plainly enjoying the scene as well, and they reclined into each other's arms, hugging and caressing. After all, this was a discussion for planning chieftains, and Breth was only a battle chieftain. He didn't have to pay close attention.

Breth's father held forth on how he had believed all along that the clans needed to be independent, and how now there was a druid to back him up.

Breth was kissing the side of Jaelle's neck, and it was all she could do to keep her gasps from being so loud that others could hear them. It took all her concentration.

Another chieftain got up. She didn't know this one's name. He clearly knew leadership, because he was absolute about waiting for attention, and he got it, even from Richard, who sat down on a nearby log and made the pose of the thinker, overdramatic fool.

The chieftain spoke in melodic tones.

"It is good to have heard the opinion of one druid. I wish to put off any decision until there is unity of opinion from them."

Richard stood up in a hurry, rolling his eyes.

"Very well. Sit tight, and I will go round everyone up."

Smiling like a kid on a snow day, Breth took Jaelle's hand and led her off into the trees, where they enjoyed each other as much as they could without doing things that really shouldn't be interrupted. But all too soon, Deoord was calling them back by name. Jaelle followed Beth back into the clearing and saw that indeed, all the Druids were standing in unity. Two dozen of them, at least.

One exceptional druid whose name she didn't know waited until all were settled before he spoke.

"We agree with Richard. We should not follow Drest. We also agree that casting him aside would destroy clan culture. Therefore, we believe Drest should submit to trial by combat."

Breth squeezed her tight and she squeezed him.

"This is perfect!" she said, beaming. "He'll be removed, and we won't have to do anything."

Breth beamed right back at her.

"We can get on with what we do want to do."

He kissed her then, right in front of everyone.

She returned his kiss voraciously, even though they had just exchanged hundreds of kisses while waiting for the Druids. People around them clapped and cheered them on. Jaelle climbed into Breth's lap so they could be closer, so she could show her love better.

That's it. That's all I want to do, love him. I've been so stupid.

She managed to pull her mouth away from his, and she nuzzled her mouth up to his ear.

"I want us to be married as soon as possible. Can these Druids do it now?"

At first, Breth stopped, in shock. But then he squeezed her tighter and nuzzled his own mouth down to her ear.

"Yes, are you ready?"

She nodded her head, but she wanted to speak and make sure he heard her.

"Yes, let's do this right now. I can't wait a minute longer!"

He held her more fiercely still, and then stood up and helped her to her feet.

But they both froze when they turned around. All the Druids were looking at Breth.

He looked from one to another, his own face in puzzlement.

"What?"

The lead Druid held out his arm toward Breth, beckoning him over.

Breth turned to Jaelle and smiled excitement, taking her along with him toward the natural focal point at the bonfire, a slight hill on one side of it.

But the head Druid spoke up.

"Leave Jaelle there, Breth. Just you come to us. Come stand with us in ceremony."

Breth stammered.

"I was just going to ask you to marry us. Isn't that what this is about?"

The druid gave Breth a solemn look.

"Nay. Nay, it is not."

The statuesque but grizzled man turned and spoke to

Jaelle directly, and she felt slightly mollified to be at least accorded the status she deserved as a warrior consort to someone who'd eventually be a planning chieftain.

"Jaelle, you need to remain there and let Breth come face this alone."

Jaelle knew she should be quiet, really she did, but her mouth...

"For the land's sake, will someone tell me what this is all about?"

By now, Breth was standing beside the lead Druid, who turned him to face all the chieftains, prodding him in the small of his back. This caused Breth to take the warrior stance: shoulders squared back, chin raised high, and legs braced for action as, with pride, he faced his parents and all the other chieftains and their families.

The lead druid waited again for quiet and got it quickly.

"This very evening, Breth will champion the clans in this momentous trial, the trial by combat of Drest."

CHAPTER 30

Jaelle jumped up to say 'No, Breth can't face Drest. I have to do it. I know all of John's weaknesses. I beat him almost every time we spar. I'm the one who should fight him!'

But a hand went over her mouth. Another snatched her arm and jerked her around. Expecting to see Richard, she prepared a particularly nasty kick and waited to site his groin. But Alasdair stood behind her, putting his finger over his lips and gesturing for her to run after him.

"John is coming, and he canna see ye yet."

Relieved it wasn't Richard but still desperate to save her love's life, she resisted, shaking her head furiously.

"I need to tell them Breth can't fight John! It should be me—"

Alasdair tugged on her arm urgently, pulling her away from the area so insistently, her feet started moving of their own accord, following him.

"Nay ye dinna," he muttered. "Trust me. I can help ye help Breth, but it will work much better if john doesna see ye till the last moment."

Trust Alasdair? Jaelle thought back to their talk on her couch and the odd experience of having the man in her mind. He had done just what he said he would. The wizened old druid was her best bet. She knew it was true, but still, she despaired when she looked back at Breth one more time and saw him surrounded.

The two dozen druids had removed Breth's baggy Pictish shorts, his form-fitting linen shirt, his scabbard and sword, and even his boots. They already had him half painted up with battle woad.

Breth's eyes met hers. He stood there resolutely confident, ever the warrior.

Without taking her eyes off Breth, Jaelle walked backward as she followed Alasdair, speaking to him out of the side of her mouth.

"You can help me help him?"

Alasdair hissed his answer, jiggling her hand almost frantically in some kind of warning.

"I can and I wull. Howsoever, Richard can and wull help Drest. We need to prepare. Now hush and turn aroond and follow me!"

She did hush and follow him, but she didn't turn around until her view of Breth was blocked by the trees.

CHAPTER 31

"Yer notice tae the museum is taken care o," said Alasdair's voice in Jaelle's mind as they went to the tournament arena the long way, through the trees. Although it was dark, she didn't stumble, and she had no choice but to attribute that to Alasdair's magic somehow.

The old grey-haired druid continued to think aloud inside her head.

"Whether or na any o us survive this day, yer friend Lauren will inform Jan, Cinnead, Vivian, and yer family that ye willna be coming back."

"Thank you," she told him in their mixed mind.

In the distant broch meadow, she heard Drest being called over to the sword-fighting tournament arena and the sounds of hundreds of excited people heading that way as well, with general calls of 'Trial by Combat!' 'Breth and Drest!'

"Shall I let Breth in on oor conversation?" was Alasdair's next thought.

"I'm afraid that would distract him."

"I wull leave it up tae ye," he thought back instantly.

The two of them had reached the torchlit arena but were still hanging back a bit, hidden in the crowd of eight clans and Drest's outcast army. As Jaelle watched Breth warm up for battle, she was overwhelmed by an urge to have him near her in some possible way before he faced death.

"You're right. Add him. Wait! Is he in yet?"

"Nay, ye caught me in time. What is it?"

"Will he be able to hear my thoughts like you, or just what I deliberately say to him?"

"Again, up tae ye."

"Maybe it's best if he hears my thoughts. They work faster than anything I could deliberately say, right?"

"Aye, but Jaelle..."

"Don't worry, I have nothing but contempt for John anymore. Breth can hear anything I have to think."

"Good."

And then Breth's voice was in her mind as well, but it wasn't just his voice. His ... essence swam about in her mind. It made her love him even more, with its purity, its nobility, its goodness.

"So," said Breth, "Alasdair tells me you've been holding back some special moves, eh?"

Her essence tangled up with his so that in their

minds, they were in each other's arms. She put on a teasing air, trying to keep his spirits up.

"I know so many moves it would take a lifetime to teach you them all."

His essence caressed hers.

"Challenge accepted."

Meanwhile in the outside world, the lead druid — Morleo was the name Breth inserted in her mind — came into the center of the torchlit arena and raised his hands. Instantly, eight hundred clans people and another three hundred outcasts fell silent and crowded around to watch.

With Breth off to one side of the arena near Alasdair and John off to the other near Richard, Morleo spoke with absolute authority.

"Drest, your authority as chieftain over all these people has been challenged, and you are called to trial by combat."

John approached Morleo with less than his late air of defiance, Jaelle noticed, and the two spoke to each other in low tones while 'Drest's men' grumbled among themselves all around and Richard stood there with his arms folded over his chest, looking smug.

Meanwhile, Deoord left the nearby clump of two dozen druids and walked up to Breth, his pasty white face looking especially primitive in the firelight coming from the circle of torches on pikes all around the arena. He checked the woad designs all over Breth and then nodded his approval. Through

Breth's ears, Jaelle heard Deoord speak softly, soothingly.

"As the challenger, this fight is on you. Do you wish to proceed?"

Jaelle couldn't help the thoughts she was having.

"Can't you just call it off, Breth?"

"And let this Drest continue degrading the honor of the clans? No."

"But—"

Alasdair's thoughts came in.

"Breth, with yer permission, I'm gaun'ae let Jaelle help ye move the way ye need tae."

Like a mental newsreel on fast forward, Alasdair quickly played snippets of all Jaelle's memories of beating John in battle, hundreds of them. To be sure, these were Society for Creative Anachronism battles with blunted wooden practice weapons and shields, but they were battles nonetheless: chaotic and full of real sword-fighting, not 'one-two-three go!' duels or fencing bouts. No.

More of Breth's warm mental energy came over Jaelle as she watched him enter the torchlit arena to stand near Morleo, awaiting the end of the druid's counseling session with Drest and the pronouncement that the trial by combat was on.

"I have no objection at all. Do your best, Jaelle. I yield to your superior range of training."

The odd feeling of being in Breth's head intensified until Jaelle had the sensation that at the same time, she was standing right here and also walking toward John.

How different it felt to be in Breth's body! He was heavier, and his limbs longer. And strong. Such strength as she had never imagined wielding. He was not so agile as she, judging by the way he moved.

This wasn't going to be easy at all.

Both of them glanced over at Drest/John in anticipation, but he was still urgently whispering with the lead druid.

"Breth, John could talk his way out of this—"

"No, Morleo won't allow it. The fight is on. Let's use this time to be as ready as we can."

"Yes, we need practice, even if it's just for an hour."

Breth looked back over toward Drest and Morleo, and she could see through his eyes that their counseling session was winding down. At the same time, Breth's thoughts asked her how long an hour was, and she pictured the sun moving across the sky with a measure in front of that, dividing the sun's day/night path into 24 equal parts.

"We have perhaps the twelfth part of an hour," he thought then.

"Better get to it. I'm going to just pretend I am you and test the balance of your sword, OK?"

"Yes, and do whatever else you want to quickly."

By exerting suggestion in his thoughts, she had him swoosh his sword a few times, testing how it was weighted, and lunge a few times, testing his reach. Next, she had him lean back as if dodging a lunge, then pivot and thrust to the side. Then he ran across the area so she could measure his strides, pivoting and coming to attention once he got there so she could feel his stance and how he balanced on the balls of his feet.

And all the while, her mind was dancing with his, exchanging surprise at how easily he moved his heavier sword for how graceful were the movements she suggested he make, and so on went their exchange of knowledge and experience.

And she felt just how much he loved her. So much. As much as she loved him. With emotional thoughts that weren't in words, he praised her, and she admired him. Their union was so beautiful, so intensely beautiful.

Alasdair put a hand on her shoulder, and she knew their practice time was up, much too soon. Breth felt it too, and he went back to his side of the arena near Morleo, watching for the druid's signal, he informed her in thought.

"Morleo!" a man called out, "Drest can't have the help of the druid Richard during the battle. Look! He's wearing a torque!"

John was still for a moment, probably listening to Richard in his mind, and then he turned on the man and then pointed at Alasdair. He looked so smug and confident. And cruel. When did he get that cruel?

"Breth has the same sort of aid, so I don't know what you're complaining about. The sides are even, now let's get this farce over with so I can get back to leading you all."

Sensing her cue, Jaelle took a few steps forward out of

the crowd with Alasdair by her side and stared at John, waiting for him to see her.

He rolled his eyes and turned back to Breth, but of course Jaelle could see him through Breth's eyes. He showed absolutely no signs of regret, nor sympathy, nor anything honorable at all. But for a fraction of a second, he had shown fear when he first saw her. But he quickly shrugged it off.

"So Breth's famous Jaelle is you. Ha! Too bad for you, they won't let you fight his battles for him, eh?"

She didn't answer, just leaned into Alasdair as if for comfort, thinking "How could I have been with such a hard-hearted person and not known it?"

Alasdair cut into her thoughts.

"People dae change. Stick wuth the business at hand. Ye need all yer concentration for this."

He was right. She concentrated on Breth — on his larger muscles, longer reach, unfamiliar weapon, and woad armor.

John was all woaded up as well, which made sense. This way, it was less likely one of them would die.

Have to stick to the bludgeoning moves, if both of us are impervious to cuts.

Morleo still held up his hands. Once he had Breth and Drest's attention as well as everyone's silence, he lowered his arms to signal the beginning of the fight.

CHAPTER 32

J ohn opened with an ordinary sword move from this time period.

Jaelle didn't try anything fancy at first, just let Breth parry in the period way.

John tried another move, and another, all period so far. Jaelle knew he was testing Breth's strength. She was getting used to it, too, and she held out hope that John was afraid, seeing how Breth's strength was so much greater than her own — which had always been more than a match for John's, with his smaller half-Filipino stature.

The two woaded warriors circled in the torchlight, half crouched and eyeing each other, until with a sneer on his face, John taunted Breth, or who he thought was only Breth.

"Afraid to make a move?"

Breth started to fall for the taunt, started an all-out lunge.

But Jaelle held him back and spoke soothingly in his mind.

"He's very quick. The way to beat him is—"

John struck like a snake. His extra-long sword spat at Breth's middle.

Jaelle bent Breth away from the jab Aikido style.

But Breth's own reflexes were strong. He moved to parry Drest's thrust. And almost got bluntly eviscerated. Only his superior strength saved him, moving the blade aside at the last instant.

"That was close."

"That worked once, Breth, but it won't work next time. He'll adapt. Let me dodge you next time!"

"I'll try."

"If only we'd had that hour of practice."

"Let's rush him this time."

Instead of answering in words or trying to control his body, Jaelle sent Breth a kinesthetic memory of how she would go about attacking John from their current relative positions.

Breth executed it perfectly, and the two shared a moment of mental triumph.

But John remembered this move too. He pivoted at the last second and moved his sword into Breth's path.

Again Jaelle tried to dodge Breth out of the way.

And again Breth's own instincts were faster. But not fast enough. The blade scraped its evil path. Only the woad saved Breth this time, preventing a deep cut, once again into his abdomen.

Alasdair's voice came in.

"Wull ye allow me tae give Jaelle brief instants o ultimate control, Breth? I ken they would serve ye in those times when ye need tae move tae the side a wee bit, as I can see in her intentions."

"Yes!"

"'Tis done."

Not a moment too soon, either, as John rushed Breth.

Jaelle was ready. She had Breth twist out of the way while at the same time jabbing at John with his sword pommel, figuring his superior size and strength would make this move count. It hit. And once you hit John, you had to just keep hitting until he was down. Otherwise, he was just too fast. So that's what she had Breth do. And it worked.

As Drest, John lay at Breth's feet, bloodied and beaten.

Jaelle thought, "You can hold him now alone. I'm coming over to talk to him as myself."

"Very well," Breth thought back to her, "but you will have to teach me all those moves, you know."

Jaelle bathed Breth's thoughts in her joy. "I have a feeling I'll be teaching the whole clan fighting for a long time, as your wife."

Her joy filled both of them as she walked up to lord it over John as herself.

John was reaching out for Breth to help him up, but

Jaelle stayed Breth's hand and stood there in his place with triumph on her face so that he would know what happened here.

"You made your bed," she said to John, "and now you have to sleep in it. You joined up all these clans along with your men, so they're our men now." She looked up and addressed the crowd. "Drest's men, you are welcome to stay if you follow our lead."

One of the outcasts threw up his hands.

"Works for me!"

Another chimed in.

"Aye!"

But then a bloodcurdling cry was heard from Richard's direction.

Grasses grew up around Breth and Jaelle, but mostly around Breth. They were tough grasses, wrapping around calf muscles and soon to be strong enough to pull the two of them off their feet.

They both re-drew their swords and hacked for all they were worth, cutting the grass as with scythes.

The grasses grew back a little farther each time they were cut, swirling around knees. And then thighs. The shorn ends of the grasses bled green goo that made bare legs itch, even Breth's woaded legs.

Alasdair was ready, however.

The grey-haired druid gestured, and a cloud of locusts emerged from thin air, gobbling up the grass faster than it could grow. Farther and farther down the green stalks the locusts ate, until they burrowed underground and raised the dirt as they chomped on grass roots.

Simultaneously, Alasdair also summoned in his hand a small flame. It emitted a deep dark cloud of smoke, which floated on its own against the wind over to Richard, swirling around him in ever tightening whorls.

The younger druid's eyes went wide in fear, and he put his hands out in front of him, pleading with Alasdair for his life.

"You can't! Celtic U forbids the smoke death!"

Alasdair shook his head and smiled in ironic sympathy.

"Richard, Richard, Richard. You were safe until you attacked Breth directly. That unlocked the forbidden spells. You know that."

With a snide grin on his face, Richard whipped the helmet out of the bag he must have been hiding with illusion and went to put it on.

But the smoke rapidly disappeared into Richard's smiling mouth, expanding his head until the helmet would not fit. And then more. And more.

Aghast at what had to happen next, Jaelle turned her head.

But Breth didn't, and through his eyes, she saw the haughty druid's head swell until it exploded, spraying brains and blood — which thankfully, Alasdair magically blocked from dirtying the crowd, meanwhile catching the helmet and holding it close to his chest.

"You cannot be allowed to keep this. You must understand," was the last thought Jaelle heard that wasn't hers before Alasdair and Breth disappeared from her mind.

She met Alasdair's eye and solemnly nodded her understanding.

There was a shocked pause as everyone took in what had happened to Richard, and then a mighty cheer went up, repeated over and over by more than a thousand who had gathered to see Breth fight Drest.

"Rrrr rrr rrr rrr!"

Amid the happy din, Morleo approached Jaelle and Breth and bowed his head ever so slightly.

"Rumor has it the two of you wish to be married."

CHAPTER 33

J aelle and Breth were entwined in each other's arms in front of the head druid, who stood there looking official. This was it. She was finally going to marry Breth! Lonely for him after that oh-so-intimate feeling of being of one mind, she clung to him and kissed him for all she was worth.

Breth reciprocated her kiss with the same ferocity.

Morleo smiled.

"Breth, as the reigning champion, you are now our leader. If Jaelle is your choice of bride, then Jaelle will be your bride. But you must choose now. We cannot have chaos in the clans, and chaos will reign so long as such an influential spot as the wife of the leader of all the chieftains is not filled. So tell me, do you wish to marry Jaelle?"

Still holding her close, Breth looked to Jaelle for her decision.

She smiled back at him, nodding.

Smiling at her as big as the grey Scottish sky, Breth answered the lead druid.

"I've wanted to marry Jaelle from the moment I first saw her."

Jaelle enjoyed a moment of pure bliss. Here was her man saying what she had longed to hear. They had defeated those who threatened the peace of the people and united ten clans in an even stronger bond that was voluntary and based on respect rather than fear. All was as she wanted.

So of course Morna stepped forward and tried to ruin it.

"What about the promise that was made to me, that I would be Breth's wife and I would help him lead his clan?"

On hearing this much, Jaelle was so annoyed, she wanted to turn around and smack the little woman. She did turn around, but the more Morna stood there talking all alone and small, the more uncomfortable Jaelle felt, until she outright felt sorry for Morna. Imagine that.

"I depended on that promise of being Breth's wife when I left my own clan to come live with his. And now my clan has been wiped out by the southern barbarians. I have nothing and no one."

Breth's mother came up, and then his father did as well, looking to Talorac and plainly expecting him to do the same. When Talorac looked off toward the hills, pretending he hadn't seen his father's beckoning look, his father spoke up.

"Regardless if one of our sons marries you, we adopt you as our daughter, Morna, with all the rights of a clan chieftain's only daughter. We will dower you if you desire to be married; we will feed, clothe, and shelter you as long as we live if you don't; and our sons will do the same as long as they live after us."

Breth's father put his arm around his wife, and both held out their other arm.

Morna went to them, and all three hugged.

Breth looked so gorgeous to Jaelle, covered in the flush of battle, that she just couldn't keep her eyes off him any longer. His eyes bored into hers so that she thought he saw into her very soul.

Morleo raised his arms for quiet again, and got it.

"Breth has defeated Drest in combat, and so he is your new chieftain."

Cheers again.

"Rrr rrr rrr rrr!"

Then, with a thousand people watching, Morleo simply joined Breth and Jaelle's hands together, raised their joined hands up, and turned them around to face everybody.

"Breth has taken Jaelle as his wife, and so she is your new chieftain's second."

Again the cheers, but all Jaelle heard was Breth groaning with anticipation as the two of them sealed the deal in front of all their cheering people with another ferocious kiss.

And then Breth carried Jaelle all the way from the

torchlit arena up to the top of the spirally staircase between the inner and outer walls of the broch to his room, where he at last laid her down.

🐚

SOMEONE HAD LEFT HONEYED MEAD AND OTHER necessities for them up there, so they didn't have to leave the room. It was mostly into the next day before they were hungry, and then Breth reluctantly pulled away from her only when his stomach growled.

"We fight fair, my love. I will have food delivered to us. Nothing but this small space shall part us for an entire honeyed moon."

Jaelle smiled up at him lazily.

"A whole month!"

Smiling and then laughing with her, Breth went to the door and called Deoord. Once he was done, he turned back to her and...

They indeed spent an entire month together in that room. Amazing. Every evening and every morning they were brought honeyed mead....

And of course Jaelle was with child. Boanne told her and Breth so together, and Breth held her tight and told her he loved her. At first, she was anxious about bearing children here, but Boanne reassured her, showing considerably more knowledge in such things than Jaelle expected in the first century. Then again, the woman was a druidess... Jaelle smiled at how silly she had been. It would all be right.

However, now that their honeyed moon was over, Jaelle was susceptible to having Breth's family members around. His father of course was overjoyed for them, and he informed them that Morna seemed satisfied with her status as his daughter, so they needn't worry about her.

Breth's mother, on the other hand...

🐚

LAUREN WOKE UP FROM THE MEMORIES ALASDAIR HAD been sharing with her, with Jaelle's permission, he insisted.

"Will Jaelle and Breth really rule over all those people?"

"Aye, but they will only dae sae in matters o war. They are leaving each clan tae rule itself for the most part, and that is tae the good."

Lauren knew there was something off about the old gray-haired druid, but she didn't care. Why should Jaelle and Kelsey and Amber have all the fun? Lauren wanted in, and Alasdair was her ticket.

🐚

JAELLE WAS ANXIOUS, AND WITH GOOD REASON. Breth's mother Almba was formidable, she held considerable sway in the community, and the first chance she got, she sent Breth on an errand so that she could spend some time alone with her new daughter-in-law.

"You are afraid of me — don't deny it — and that is to the good." Almba's chest filled up with pride and she lifted her chin before returning to her neutral diplomatic stance. "My son has very few who will look out for him now that he has risen so high. Most of the chieftains will envy him his power, and some will try to take it away. He needs a wife who will always stand by him, oftentimes in battle..."

Jaelle was thinking 'I'm the best one for that.' In fact, she opened her mouth to say so.

But Breth's mother put her hand over Jaelle's mouth.

"I know, Jaelle. I know you can fight beside him, and that you will. That is the only reason I did not fight harder against your marriage. You need to understand how things work in this time. On the one hand, even though Morna's clan is gone, the other chieftains have known her all her life. She has strong allies among them. On the other hand, the only alliance you bring is with yourself — and perhaps with the druid Alasdair. I have decided that is enough. Don't let me down."

Almba's eyes bore into Jaelle's almost as powerfully as Breth's had, but with only a tiny fragment of the affection he had for her. This was a command, and a stare to enforce that command, and a promise of severe bodily harm should she not obey the command.

Jaelle's mouth surprised her with something good this time.

"You needn't worry. I genuinely love your son. I do have his back, always. I will stand by him to the end. I already have in what might've been the end. You needn't fear."

Breth's mother softened then. She actually smiled at Jaelle — and then hugged her.

"I am convinced this is true." And then she turned to the door of Jaelle and Breth's room and called out, "Enter."

The door opened, and in came Morna. Looking like she'd been crying, she knelt at Jaelle's feet and bowed low.

"I accept you as my chieftain's wife and my leader and my better. I will resist you no more. I will only do things to help you, for the land's sake."

Almba put Jaelle's hand on Morna's head and then nodded toward the crying woman, moving her lips.

Jaelle nodded and turned to the woman kneeling in front of her.

"I accept your fealty, but I deny that I'm your better."

Both the other women gasped, looking at her in wonder.

Jaelle went on.

"I know that our society has betters, but I consider everyone equal. We hold positions that are unequal, and we must respect the position, but in my mind and my heart, all people are equal. Rise, Morna. I hope we shall be sisters."

Morna raised her head, eyes loaded with fear, and

Jaelle realized there was a misunderstanding.

"Not on the battlefield, to be sure. I don't expect you to become a warrior."

Morna relaxed and breathed again.

Jaelle gave the small beautiful woman a tentative friendly smile.

"I wish for there to be love between us, and nothing else."

The tiniest smile of gratefulness appeared on Morna's face. It wasn't much at all, but Jaelle saw it and nodded. For now, it was enough.

TALORAC FELT ANXIOUS ABOUT THIS MEETING. BEING summoned to the sacred grove always meant preparing for battle. He was in no way prepared to make the acquaintance of the woman he found there. Deirdre was beautiful, and a warrior, and from the way she was flitting around the grove, she was the most powerful druid he had ever heard of in his life.

THE NEXT BOOK, TIME OF THE DRUIDS, CONTAINS Talorac and Deirdre's complete romance with happily ever after — and more of Breth and Jaelle's adventures with the Gaels and the Romans. To find out more about Deirdre, read Seumas.

Jaelle thinks she dreamed her time travel until she sees a piece of Hadrian's Wall with graffiti she created

Time of the Druids

Deirdre and Galdus travel to the time of Hadrian's Wall

Leif

Lauren and Galdus trick two friends into time traveling

Taran

Lauren surrenders to Galdus - or does she?

Luag

Lauren's friend Katherine takes on a laird's court

As Cherise Kelley:

Dog Aliens 1, 2 & 3: A Dog Story

My Dog Understands English!

How I Got Him to Marry Me

High School Substitute Teacher's Guide

Made in the USA
Middletown, DE
08 September 2021

47899194R00123